Take a deep breath, pick yourself up, dust yourself off, and start all over again. – Frank Sinatra

Prologue

The scent is all wrong. Roses and maxed-out air conditioning fill the room and my nostrils, and my stomach flips for the tenth time. The mass of visitors in black passes before me in a blur. I find it hard to focus on any one face. Their words are all the same empty apologies, with variation only in vocal quality. Some hold back tears, others are stronger. All fail to bring me comfort.

I have two dear friends on my right side and a stoic shell of a husband on my left. Even so, I am alone. The realization of how alone I am hits me like a punch in the chest. Each breath becomes labored. They grow shorter and shorter while the top of my black dress that I will never wear again seems to tighten and cut off all air. I reach out, oddly to my right side only, and grab the arms that reach back in slow motion. The floor is made of crimson red carpet. It rises slowly to meet me as the rest of my world goes black.

1 Exhaustion

Of course it would be raining.

Isn't that always how the weather is on bad days? Or maybe it's usually sunny in an attempt to be ironic and make you even more miserable. Either way, it's raining today. It's storming even. At least I don't have to make an excuse to avoid going outside.

Today is the first day in my new, tiny, lousy apartment. The walls are the shade of buttermilk, and the light covers are older than I am. This is the type of apartment someone should rent while in college and living off of noodles, schnapps, and loans. The chipped floors are littered with boxes that will take days to sort, but thankfully, I can't sleep for more than a few hours at a time anyhow. I have plenty of quiet time to unpack all of the things I own in the world.

I don't mean to sound bitter. This has just been a very hard year. I know lots of people go through trying times, but that does not make it any easier for me. My friends have been great, but the fact that they get to go back to their families at night is not lost on me. My evening company will be these boxes for as far into the future as I dare to daydream.

Crash!

My eyes fly open while I simultaneously wince from the flashes of lightening. I guess I did fall asleep at some point. It is still storming outside, and thanks to the trumpet-like thunder and jarring lightening, I am now completely awake. The clock's red lights pierce through my dark bedroom, telling me that it is only 4:15am. *Ugggghhhh*. If I have learned anything over the past few months, I know that there is no use trying to fall back asleep now. I may as well crawl out of bed.

Where are my shoes? I swear, I'll finish unpacking tonight.

One good thing about my new apartment is that there is a gym on my street that is open 24 hours, including 4:15 in the barely morning. After digging through the unpacked boxes scattered across my floors to find anything that resembles workout clothes, I am able to escape my quiet cell for a half hour and be around other people. I wouldn't say normal people though. Who chooses to be at the gym, or anywhere really, this early?

I blink at the bright lights in my building's narrow hallway, head down two flights of stairs, cross the still-dark and mostly empty street, and make it into Stride's Gym. Even though it's a high-end gym filled with sleek, shiny equipment, sanitizing stations, and a persistent *thump thump* of whatever the music trend is now, the pre-dawn look of this place is not doing a lot to boost my morale.

I trudge through 30 minutes on the elliptical and listen to the swishing of my legs trying to get back into some type of healthy routine. The weeks of takeout binge eating mixed with bouts of depression-induced nausea has done little for my wellness. When I've put in my half hour of cardio, I feel marginally better and I think I'm ready to conquer my boxes. I tell myself I'll empty at least five of them today. Maybe four...

I dash back to my apartment and I wonder if it will ever stop raining. Once I'm back inside and able to find a towel to dry off from the rain, the first thing that hits me, like always, is how quiet it is. I need some type of noise. I am grateful that cable was one of the first things I set up when I found this place. I find some new Indie music station in the 400-something channels and prep myself for the tasks ahead. I've got this.

After only two boxes in as many hours, I bargain with myself to unpack just one more. I'm not sure that I can handle another thing that reminds me of my ex-husband. (Will the *ex-* ever seem like a normal thing to say?) I choose the lesser of two evils and work on the box that I took from my mother's house after she died. I had been able to go through almost all of her things, but when my marriage started to fail, I stopped before I got to this box. "Now is as good of a time as any", I say out loud to myself for motivation.

This small box opens with a familiar but musty smell. *Mom. I miss you so much.* This box just has a few of her clothes, and I know will probably end up just putting them right back in to pack away and save. I can't imagine getting rid of anything else of hers, especially now when I already feel so lonely. Her favorite blue and white polka dot sweatpants that she used to sleep in are on the top. She loved pajamas! I would buy her new ones for her birthday every year. Some were warm and cozy for the snowy Utah winters, and some were just shorts and a t-shirt for her to lounge in when it was warmer. She always kept this faded pair with the polka dots on hand. It's what I picture her wearing when I'd stay over to visit when Jared was away on "business".

Next is her long red pullover that she loved to wrap herself into when it was especially cold. Under this is....*what is this?* I guess it's possible that I've just forgotten about the sweatshirt, I think to myself, though

I'm confident I've never seen it before. It is a light cream color with green and yellow stripes around the cuffs. The sweatshirt is pretty retro and very soft from time and wear. Why would she have this with all of her favorite clothes when I can't ever remember seeing it before?

But she must have loved it because it smells just like her. The soft lily musk that not only dominated her perfume shelf also diffused her home and garden. I find myself putting the sweatshirt on and wrapping up in the comfort, scent, and warmth of my mother, despite my apparent wardrobe memory lapse. Oh how I long for her to be with me. She would help me with my heartache, just like she always has. I try to imagine her stroking my light blonde curls until I am hypnotized and soothed to sleep by the rhythm of her fingers and the hum of her song.

Suddenly, I'm exhausted. I guess the lack of sleep, the early morning, and the emotional and literal unpacking have finally gotten to me. I don't even care that it's 8:00 on a Saturday morning or that the sun is finally coming out. As an insomniac, I am embracing this exhaustion.

2 Almost certainly nothing at all

"What's wrong my little angel?," I hear my dad say. "Don't cry. Everything is going to be just fine." I'm not quite sure why I'm crying, but I hear my mother start to cry too, even though she isn't here. She must be in her bedroom down the hall. My five-year-old self starts to tremble. My mother's wailing grows louder, but my father doesn't go to find her. He doesn't even look up or give any sign that he hears her. I need to find her to help her, but where is she? Why won't dad go to her and comfort her? Sitting here on this old, lumpy couch won't help my mother, so I run to look for her. I'm in one room and through another. There are so many doors and an ever-expanding amount of rooms, but my mother isn't here. I can't find my mom. The crying will not stop.

Finally, through a labyrinth that is somehow my childhood home and at the same time a carnival "fun" house, I see her. She is rocking on her old, creaking rocking chair, hugging my father's sweatshirt, and sobbing. Where did my dad go? Why didn't he follow me or even try to find mom? Why are we all alone?

Gasping, I sit up too quickly and have to lay back down to avoid falling over. It's only 8:36am but at least I got a little bit of sleep. I was never a good sleeper, but having my mother die and then six months later walking in on my husband with a seductress named Monica, I've all but given up on a good night's sleep.

Monica. The name offends every one of my senses, and I feel nauseated. It's best not to even think of her, I tell myself. I know it is Jared's fault since he was the one to ignore his vows, our vows, but the thought of the other woman always makes me dizzy and sick.

The doctor says stress is causing my nightmares and that they will probably stop once I am able to relax. I sat in a cold exam room, far from relaxed and wearing only a paper robe when she offered me a sedative. I know it is ok for me to take something. Many people do. But I was once able to stand on my own, and I want to be that strong person again.

As usual, I keep replaying my dream over and over until I realize that there is more than the obvious loss and sadness that is bothering me. I replay the dream in my mind, recalling as many details as I can muster. My mind catches on the last scene before I bolted awake. I remember my mother, inconsolable and clutching a cream-colored sweatshirt. Feeling steadier, I run to the box labeled "Mom's Clothes" and dig through the pile inside. Once my fingers touch the worn fabric, I know I have it. I pull the sweatshirt out and examine it top to bottom. I turn it over in my hands and comb my memory for any hidden glimpse, any small recollection to place this discovery.

I think to myself, "Was this old thing really my father's sweatshirt, or am I just putting this detail into my subconscious because it is new to me?". I'm sure my mind is just trying to connect dots and make sense of all of the recent changes in my life, because there is no way that I remember something my father wore all those years ago. My father died when I was five. That was twenty-five years ago.

Many people have tragic lives. There are stories of starving and being homeless, being abused, never having parents long enough to form a memory, and so many other, horrible existences. Even so, I feel wrecked. My dad died when I was five, my mother when I was 29, and now I am divorced at 30. How can I possibly get through this?

I do my best to remember what my doctor advised, and I start to list all of the good things I have: I am healthy. I have enough food. I have a job that pays the bills. I have my best friends, Zanna and Emily. I will be ok. My breathing calms, and I decide it's time to forget these dreams and memories and watch TV for a while.

I wrap up in what I will consider my mom's sweatshirt, breathe in what is left of her scent, and try to get comfortable on the couch. It's amazing how I can have so many channels and yet not have anything to watch. Then I cynically remember that it is an early, sunny, Saturday morning and everyone else is outside being happy. Cheerful families are probably below my windows right now, holding hands and skipping off to the park. This thought makes me certain that I will stay right here on this couch, no matter how lumpy it is, and not move for a while.

This lasts for about five minutes when the sweatshirt just will not cooperate. There is a tiny jab on my right side every time I move an inch. I give up and move from my cocoon of blankets to see what in the world continues to poke me. I reach into the pocket and find an old, yellowed envelope with no writing on the outside. *This does not happen*, I think to myself. *Did my mom somehow send a letter from beyond to tell me all of the life lessons I'm supposed to learn? Will she tell me that it will all be ok? That I will be happy again? That I will I stop feeling so lonely?*

I am a basket of nerves, and my hands start to sweat. I open the envelope so slowly and carefully that it takes me almost three full minutes. I do not want to ruin any other-worldly power or luck that I am touching right now. Once I've finally loosened the seal, I can see that it's not a letter, but a picture. I am so disappointed. I'm not even sure who these people are.

Wow Lydia, you are really losing it. Did you really think your dead mother wrote you an encouragement letter? Apparently I did.

Pushing through the disappointment, I wonder what is so special about this picture, sealed in a crumbling envelope and tucked inside a mysterious 1970's style sweatshirt in a box of my dead mother's favorite things. On the back, it reads "Greg and Alex, 1985. Our new home." Greg was my father's name. This must be a picture of him, but who is Alex? My dad died in 1985. *What is this?*

Only after I see the name Greg can I easily see that the picture is, of course, of my dad. His sandy blonde hair that is the precise shade of mine is casually swept to the side. His emerald eyes shine through the picture and over decades to spark my few memories of him from my early childhood. He is with a little boy, apparently Alex based on the writing, posing by a moving truck and a bright blue mailbox. The house in the background is a charming cottage style house with white shutters and a door painted the same shade of blue as the mailbox. The trees are just starting to bloom, so it might be early spring. My dad died right before Christmas that year.

I don't have a lot of memories of my dad. I remember being sad when he died, and I remember my mother crying a lot. We had a quiet Christmas that year with store-bought shortbread cookies. Mom couldn't quite muster the energy to do the whole day-long tradition of cookie-cutting, baking, and elaborate decorating like we usually did, but she tried her best to make me happy. We had ribboned presents, and our plaid stockings were hung above the fireplace, even if we never did light the fire. It was a subdued winter that year, but we got through it together.

After that Christmas, we really never talked about my dad. We had a few pictures of him holding me when I was a baby or of the two of us playing together in my room. I remember one picture where he was looking at my chubby baby cheeks. His smile was so proud! My mom answered my questions when I asked about him, but that was really it. She didn't bring him up herself, and I eventually asked fewer and fewer questions. It was just the two of us, and we had a good life. Mom was a strong woman, and she taught me to be strong too. At least I'm trying to be. It is so much harder without her here.

I decide that I am just not able to handle this picture right now. It is too confusing. It is almost certainly nothing at all, but I cannot think about it with a clear mind at this moment. I'll come back to it later. For now, I think I'll have some grilled cheese for lunch, watch something, anything on TV, and then I swear, I'll unpack those boxes.

3 I've run out of luck

The sun is shining through the gap in the window blinds, hitting me square in the face. This must be my cue to get up off the couch. It is amazing how time can seem to go so quickly and so slowly at the same time. It is almost 4:00 and I don't have much to say for my day, as if it mattered much. I have all evening and night to be here by myself in this shabby apartment.

After another hour goes by with absolutely nothing getting accomplished, loud, obnoxious knocking erupts on my door. Before I can react, I hear Zanna's loud voice: "Out of bed Lydia! We're celebrating tonight!" I can't help but laugh out loud. When I get the deadbolt and chain unlatched on the rickety door that definitely does not open to a beautiful front yard like mine used to, Emily and Zanna crash in with champagne, ice cream, and pizza. These are the essentials.

"What are you wearing?," Zanna asks, her upper lip curled in mock disgust.
"Leave her alone. She's allowed to wear pajamas or whatever old clothes she finds lying around," says Emily. The way she says "old" sounds more sympathetic than I think she intends.
"Thanks guys. I swear, I'll wear real clothes tomorrow."

"Perfect. You'll wear real clothes when we go out for dinner tomorrow. We need to make sure you're eating actual food before going back to work. None of this take out, deep fried garbage that you've been living off of," Emily smiles. My eyes shift to the "actual food" that my friends have brought, and Emily laughs knowingly.

"What would I do without you two?" I open the bottle of champagne and rummage through boxes looking for plates.
"Stop that!" Zanna reaches into her bag and pulls out confetti covered, pink paper plates with matching plastic cups. "You do not have to do any cleaning after this housewarming party."

Standing in my tiny new apartment around my even tinier, more rickety kitchen table, the three of us try to solve the world's problems together. This could have been a really terrible night trying to get settled into my new life, but my best friends always know exactly what to do and when to do it to help me piece my life back together. We cry and laugh and badmouth Jared. I can't even repeat what is said about the horrid Monica.

All night, my hand keeps wondering back to the envelope in my pocket. I should probably tell Emily and Zanna, or at least I should take it out of my pocket and put it back into the box of my mother's things. I should really take off this old sweatshirt and put something clean on, but I don't do any of these things. The envelope brushes my hand every time I pull the sweatshirt around me. I decide to keep my mouth shut about it because it is probably nothing. It's probably just a picture of my dad when he and my mom were helping some friend's family move. My mom snapped a picture and somehow it was forgotten about until now. Maybe the sweatshirt even belonged to my dad's friend. But it isn't my mom's handwriting on the picture...

"Lydia?," Emily asks, jarring me from my reverie.

"Oh, sorry guys." My daydreaming must have shown on my face.

"Maybe I've had one too many glasses of champagne."

"Are you going to be ok?," asks Emily with concern written all over her face.

"Of course she's going to be ok." Zanna breaks in and looks right at me. "You are strong, beautiful, and smart. Jared will come to his senses, but by then, you will have already moved on. Maybe not with another person, but with your life. You can do this."

"Thanks guys. You are amazing, and I'm so lucky to have you both. I think I'm just tired."

"Good! Sleep is exactly what you need now," Emily says.

We throw away our fancy housewarming party plates and clean up my 5' by 5' kitchen. I think about how lucky I am to have Emily and Zanna, and I promise myself to get out of my sweats and meet them for dinner tomorrow.

Once they're gone, the quiet sets in again. It's amazing how lonely I am when I'm alone and how crowded I feel when I'm with people. It reminds me of what love felt like: too much and not enough at the same time. I do not like being on the other end of this. Luckily, the night's distractions may have worn me out enough to be able to sleep, even if it's just for a few hours. I push myself to brush my teeth and shuffle to bed with my ears buzzing from champagne mixed with the silence surrounding me. I curl up in my bed and try to fall asleep, conscious of the pricking coming from the envelope in my pocket.

The clock glows 4:45am and my head throbs. Regardless, I'm grateful to know that I slept 15 minutes longer than yesterday. Baby steps. I trudge to the bathroom and drink right from the faucet. Today will be a good day. I make my first real breakfast in months, a decent breakfast of dip eggs and rosemary toast, and then I'm able to unpack two whole boxes. Baby steps.

By 9:00, my headache is gone and the quiet starts to get to me again. I am overwhelmed by all that I have to do to get settled into my apartment combined with the desire to do absolutely nothing. I decide to head to the gym, especially since it's a decent hour and normal people with normal schedules might actually be there. I grab my shoes, headphones, and the same workout gear from yesterday, and I plan to zone out for a bit. Today, I'll run to the gym! Sure, it's only next door, but those stairs count for something, right?

Thirty-five minutes later, I'm finished with another elliptical session and am huffing and puffing, trying to run back up my stairs. I guess a few times back at the gym doesn't exactly make me "in shape," but it's something.

While I was working out and listening to a battle between music that was too loud and my thoughts that were even louder, I gave in to daydreaming. For once, I wasn't thinking about Jared, wishing and at the same time begging him not to see the extreme error in his ways and call to implore me to come back. No. Today, I was thinking about my dad.

My memories brought me right back to my childhood room. The pictures on my nightstand showed a handsome 30-something blonde haired man. Out of the window, I could see him grinning while he pushed a four-year-old me on a swing. It was in our backyard, the sun was shining, and dandelions speckled the grass. Some people think of them as weeds, but they have always been flowers to me. I loved to pick them and give bouquets by the handful to my favorite people. I remember picking a particularly lush bunch and walking proudly up to my first grade teacher, Mrs. Roberts. She was not nearly as thrilled as I expected her to be, barely touching them before putting the bundle on the picnic table where they stayed, even after we went inside. Later I found out she was allergic.

I was so happy when my dad was home and would play with me. I had my neighborhood friends that I would run around with, but when my dad was home, I wanted to be all his. I used to love when he threw a baseball all the way up, I swear, through the clouds. I would ask him to do it again and again while I failed again and again at trying to catch it. I don't remember him being gone too often, but my mom said he spent most of his time at work. He did a good job of making our time together count.

He traveled for business and would spend weeks at a time away. He dazzled me with his stories of Chile's snow during our summer, Copenhagen's hordes of bicycles clogging the streets, looking over the Champs-Élysées of Paris at night, and wherever else in the world that his job took him. He's probably the reason I'm in sales now, though I don't travel nearly as much or as exotically as he used to. Maybe that's why I didn't have too hard of a time adjusting after he was gone. I know I was sad and I am positive that I missed him and our play dates, but my mom and I managed. She never let me feel lonely, even though she worked full time and often part-time at a bookstore or diner in the evenings.

Despite my dad's death and absence as I grew, I had a good childhood. Why does my adulthood seem to be so much of the opposite? Did I use up all of my happiness? Twenty-nine good years and that's it?   With this new, silent life surrounding me now, it sure seems like I've run out of luck.

Once back in my apartment, I turn on my laptop and wait for several minutes for it to start up. I really need a new computer. I search for "Gregory Burke 1954". Sometimes I wonder what the connection is between what is searched and what the internet spits out. I guess someone named Gregory Burke worked for a department store at some time. Either that or the internet just knows I need some new furniture and decided to remind me. There's a Gregory Burke who has a Facebook page (he's my age), one who works at a bank (he could be my grandfather), one who apparently wins a lot of marathons (I used to be in shape!), one who is a legal assistant and posted his résumé online, one who is a musician, and on and on. Gregory Burke is not as unique of a name as I thought it was.

Nothing seems related to my dad, the one Gregory Burke I'm actually looking for. I didn't really expect to find anything, but after an hour of searching and following endless leads, I feel defeated. The internet has information on everyone, everything, and every place, but I can't even find an obituary for Gregory Burke, born 1954, residence Utah. My dad was important to me, but it sure seems like the rest of the world disagrees.

With that thought lingering, I am motivated to finish unpacking. I cannot allow myself to start wallowing in the death of my father all these years later. I am too occupied with one hundred other disappointments and sorrows right now. If I start thinking about all of these things, I'll never get myself out of this apartment. Plus, I have dinner plans with Zanna and Emily, and I need to prepare myself for tomorrow's day back at the office. I took a long weekend off to move, but I don't want to waste any more vacation days stuck in this cardboard box of an apartment feeling so utterly alone.

I think everyone must always have at least one box left unpacked after a move. I can't say that I have ever completely finished emptying all of my boxes: not in my college dorm, my first apartment, or my home with Jared. So when I realize it is 4:30 and I start to reach for my last box of worldly possessions, I decide to call it a successful day and head to the shower.

4 Thai Food

My friends and I are meeting at A Taste of Thai at 6:00 tonight. For the first time in a while, I'm actually excited, maybe even happy! I shower and head to my freshly stocked closet to pick out my favorite pair of skinny jeans, purple stilettos, and a white top. I rummage through my jewelry to complete the outfit with a long colorful necklace and simple diamond earrings. At 5:50 I grab a light jacket and start to bolt out the door and down the stairs. My reflection beckons from the newly hung mirror on my wall and the bags under my eyes make me grimace. As I'm hobbling down the stairs, the slight pain in my legs reminds me of my early morning exercise. A year ago I wouldn't have blinked twice at a short 35 minute cardio session, but this twinge makes me wonder if I'll ever get back to the person I used to be.

The taxi drops me off only a few minutes late, and my favorite ladies are waiting for me inside with a very full glass of Sauvignon Blanc. The nice thing about a BYOB restaurant is you don't have to wait around for someone to bring you your drink. I'm pretty sure there are two glasses of wine crammed to the brim of my oversized glass.

"There she is! Out of her pajamas and looking spectacular!" yells Zanna, a little too loud. My face must turn red because she laughs and shoves my drink in my hand.

"You look much better today than you did in those musty sweats from last night. How are you feeling?," Zanna asks.

"Today was a productive day. I got to the gym, finished unpacking (close enough), and even put on makeup." I say. Baby steps.

Emily, always the kind one, says, "And you look ravishing! Welcome back to the real world."

That couldn't be further from the truth, but at least I'm fooling someone. I'm uncomfortable in my clothes and wonder if I'm trying too hard. I have the familiar feeling that I want to be alone, to wallow.

"One step at a time. I still feel like a zombie, and I haven't slept a full night in months, but this is a good start," I lie. "I am *starving*," I say in an effort to change the topic. "I'm tired of fast food and delivery. Let's order before I eat these napkins."

Thai food is one of my most favorite cuisines. I hadn't tried too many different restaurants with Jared because he was fairly picky (spaghetti with red sauce was a staple in his diet), but Zanna, Emily, and I have always loved to come to A Taste of Thai. The persistent crowd, cheesy decorations, and most of all, the mouth-watering smell of curry and hot peppers always puts a smile on my face and an immediate grumble of hunger in my stomach.

Emily always defaults to Pad Thai with shrimp. The onions, eggs, bean sprouts, and peanut flavors come together perfectly. Zanna is more adventurous and doesn't have a go-to. Tonight she picks Drunken Noodles with level three spiciness. "Bring her another water and some bread with that please!" I'm teasing her, but not completely.

Zanna always thinks she can handle spicy food, but level three spiciness at a Thai restaurant is a whole new experience! She will need all the help she can get. I decide on Panang Curry. Coconut milk makes everything better. Add basil and bell peppers over rice and I'm in heaven.

I aim to go slow with my double pour of wine tonight since I have to work tomorrow, but it's hard not to get sucked into a night of fun with two amazing friends. When our food comes with nearly two servings per meal, Emily and I dig in immediately while Zanna chokes down her first too-big bite. And just like that, half of her water is gone. "I told you!" I laugh. "I just choked. This is not too spicy. Try it!"

As always, we all dig into each other's plates, family-style. Zanna's dish is much too spicy, but she somehow makes it through most of her meal. I always plan to order the fried ice cream for dessert, but as usual, I am bursting at the seams. Between the three of us, we have leftovers for lunch tomorrow that will be a mixture of all of our noodles, rice, and an assortment of spices. There is almost nothing better than a good lunch to look forward to to get you through a Monday morning at work.

"They're going to have to roll me out of here. I'm so full!," says Emily. "Me too. If I'm going to keep eating like this, I'm definitely going to have to stick to my new gym habit."

Zanna looks up. "You're starting to work out again? Great! That will be my motivation to get back into it, too. We'll motivate each other to stick with it, and that will keep you from going mad inside that so-called 'apartment'." She uses air quotes to describe my new home and then shifts her gaze to stare Emily down. "Em, there's no reason to try and resist. You're committed now too."

Sigh. "Of course I am. I don't think Derrick will mind me being gone a few mornings each week if it means I'll be able to fit into my bikini for the next summer."

"You are ridiculous. You're beautiful and you know it." I roll my eyes. "We're not going to obsess over bikinis. We want to be healthy, eat all of the food we can fit without showing it, and give me something other than Jared to think about. Right?"
"Right" they say in unison.
"So it's settled. We'll meet at the gym tomorrow morning?" Zanna asks.

Emily looks startled. "Whoa, I need to ease back into this. I'll probably still be digesting this meal until tomorrow night anyhow. Can we start Tuesday?"

And so it's settled. I hail my cab and head home for a quiet night that hopefully involves sleep. Having trouble sleeping so often makes just the thought of going to bed anxiety-provoking. As soon as I walk in the door, I turn on the TV to have some noise in the apartment and pack up my leftovers to take with me in the morning. I take my time getting my clothes and work bag ready and plan, once again, my new route to work. If I get up at 6:00, I can get to the gym and back by 7:00, and then be ready to leave and walk to work by 8:00.

I set my alarm for 6:00 and almost laugh out loud. I hope I can sleep at all tonight. If I sleep until 6:00, I'll just skip work to celebrate it! Of course, when I run out of things to do and have no choice but to lie down and pray for sleep, my imagination starts up.

There's the usual thoughts of Jared. I wonder what he is doing right now and if he is even thinking about me. I want him to be hurting more than I am, but more than that, I want to not care what he is doing or feeling. He's probably with Monica. My stomach churns at the thought. I had such a fun night with my friends. I felt so strong, but just like that, one thought of Jared brings me back to square one. After an hour of tossing and turning and replaying the last few months of my marriage, I realize I will never get to sleep if I keep this up.

What else can I think of? I look to my left and even in the black of my room after midnight, I can see my mother's cream sweatshirt. My mind's eye goes right to the picture in the pocket. Why do I keep thinking about this? It can't be anything of importance because my mom would have told me about it. But then again, why would she keep it after all these years if it was just a random picture. She didn't even keep pictures of my dad up around the house when I was growing up. I always assumed it was just too painful and wouldn't have let her move on if she saw his face every day. Why would she keep a picture of him and a little boy I've never seen before?

Around and around, questions and scenarios swirl through my mind. Like sheep, nonsense thoughts eventually put me to sleep. The next time I roll over, a red "4:45" stares back at me. It may have only been a few hours of sleep, but it's better than nothing and there's no sense in laying here anymore. I shut off my optimistic 6:00 alarm and trudge to the bathroom. I am not thrilled to be going to the gym with the other crazies today, but it sure beats the darkness and solitude of my bedroom.

The gym is a little more crowded than it was this weekend in the very early morning. I'm reminded that it is a work day and many of these other go-getters are up and getting their work week started on the right foot. I so wish I had another day to wallow in my pajamas. But there are bills to pay, and they need to be paid from only one paycheck now. I try to catch on to the enthusiasm of the others around me to prepare myself for the work day ahead. It doesn't work.

The stairs back up to my apartment seem at least two stories longer than they used to be. My head pounds from exhaustion. I start up the coffee maker and take a cold shower to try to wake myself up. My body is instantly covered with a million goose bumps. I feel more awake, but also more sad. I'm cold, alone, and I hurt. My legs are sore from my workout and every inch of me is sore from heartache. I give in and sob in my shower. It has been a while since I let myself cry, and the floodgates have opened. It is like all of the tears I held in over the past several days are coming out, along with tears for my mom and tears for my dad. I have never felt so alone in my entire life. I can barely catch my breath.

After too long in the cold water, I realize I'm shivering from the temperature as much as from the emotional outpouring. I turn up the heat and gasp as the warmth returns to my body. My overly long shower puts me exactly back on my schedule to get to work on time. I pull myself together, have some flavorless oatmeal, grab my lunch (which I remind myself is fantastic leftovers and motivation to make it until noon), ignore the reflection in the mirror, and head down the two flights of stairs.

The almost-fall scent of the morning and the hot coffee in my mug help to ground me. I'm able to walk to work now since I could pick an apartment that was best for me, not best for the "us" that used to be. This is the start of a new week and a new life. I take a deep breath, and walk through the waking city to my office.

5 Four Hundred Sycamore

It is hard to focus back at the office. Just like at the apartment, I keep watching the minutes tick by. At least here, phone calls and emails need to be answered and attempts at small talk with those offering sales opportunities need to be made. It's amazing how the world goes on, even while my life is in the midst of turmoil. In the last several months, I've often been astonished that the sun still rises. I can't understand when I hear people having normal conversations at restaurants and on the sidewalks. Don't they know that my world has fallen apart? And yet. And yet ringing phones need to be answered and blinking inboxes need to be attended.

I took this job 8 years ago to get my foot in the door of the sales world. The company sells appliances, and my job is to ensure as many stores as possible in the tri-state area stock as many refrigerators, chest freezers, and whatever other household must-haves I can convince them to take. The job pays the bills and my coworkers are amicable, though distant. There are pros and cons to this. There is almost no chance of work place drama, but that seems to go hand-in-hand with almost no chance of knowing more than someone's first name and their four-digit extension.

This was my first job right out of college, and my mom and I were so proud that I was able to land it. I envisioned working up to a management position and then changing to a bigger company with more exotic products and definitely a more exotic location. After a year, I got a small retention bonus with the promise of another when I hit three years. By that point, I had a good client base and work was easy. I'm not overly challenged, I have a stable job, and I'm not starving or in debt. That is more than many people can ask for.

When the minute hand finally hits 5:00, I picture an old cartoon whistle blowing signaling the end to another nine-to-five. I gather my things and rush out with all of my co-workers. The fake smile I keep plastered to my face seems to be working, and no one sympathetically asks me how my day was. I keep my head down and rush home.

Once home, I wonder what the rushing was all about. There's no one here to share my day with, never mind how uneventful it was. I make an easy dinner of macaroni and cheese with peas and use the paper plates from Emily and Zanna. The only thing to do now is watch reruns of something not too melancholy and also not too happy or romantic until I convince myself to lay down and try to sleep.

Fall turns to winter and the daylight hours get shorter, but somehow, the days seem just as long as ever. I've gotten myself into a routine of work, eat, and sleep, with the occasional night out with Zanna and Emily or early morning at the gym. Sometimes, my friends even keep their word and join me for a workout. Work is work, but it's something to concentrate on. Having a routine helps me to go through the motions, but it's not much of a life. I need more, but getting myself up off of the ground and surviving a day at a time is as much as I can do right now.

Today is Friday, and I am once again torn by the relief of having a few days off and the fear of hours on end without a plan or people to spend them with. The hum of the refrigerator reminds me that I do have one task for the weekend, and that is to go grocery shopping. Going to Marty's Market isn't exactly the exciting Friday night I would have planned for myself five years ago, but this is my life now. I change into my comfortable jeans, run a brush through my hair, and slump down the stairs, cloth shopping bags in tow.

Now that I am flying solo for nearly everything, it seems that all I can see are happy families enjoying time together. They are everywhere, even at the grocery store on a cold Friday night. Husbands are picking out racks of ribs while wives choose the best fruits and vegetables to add to their colorful, healthy carts. Well-behaved children are picking out their cereal for the week ahead. They all smile and laugh while I feel a knife ripping through my gut, making me physically nauseous. It's all I can do to throw my meager supply of food into my basket and run back to my solitude.

With my head down, I barrel out of the sliding glass doors and right into the chest of a middle-aged blonde, groceries scattering along the sidewalk. "In a hurry?" asks the man as he helps me collect my week's sustenance. We are able to get everything in one handful each, reminding me again how small my life has become. When he looks up, I'm unable to speak. What is wrong with me? "Are you ok?", he asks with a worried expression when I don't answer. I shake my head, confused by how shocked I feel and clear my throat. "I'm so sorry", I say, and I grab my food out of his hands and run back to my apartment, humiliated.

Unpacking my groceries and replaying the encounter, I still can't place why I was so startled. The only reason I can find is how distracted I was with the happy families surrounding me at the store. I need to get a grip. Later, I stand in the shower for a long time, letting the hot water run off of my body and swirl down the drain. When I'm finally pruned and ready to get out, I find my polka dotted pajamas, wrap up in blankets on the couch, and try not to think about my mom or Jared.

I startle awake on the couch, as is my new habit. It's after midnight, and the apartment is dark other than the TV playing reruns of Seinfeld. I dreamt of my dad again. We were both on the floor, picking up the contents of my upturned Beauty and the Beast backpack that I had in the first grade. There were Lisa Frank pencils and scented fruit-shaped erasers, pink notebooks and colorful pens, countless coloring books and crayons. I think about how my dreams always seem to have a never-ending element to them. And then it hits me. The blonde man from Marty's Market reminded me of my dad. I was looking for comfort, for family, and my mind tried to create this in a stranger that I almost knocked into the street. He didn't even look like my father all that much. But who knows what my dad would look like now, over two decades since the last time I saw him.

I wipe the sleep out of my eyes and grab the picture of my mom and me that I keep on the end table. I had just graduated college, and she was so proud. With a limited income that comes with a single-parent household, I wasn't sure if college would ever be an option for me. My mom told me to never let our current situation dictate my future. She helped me fill out scholarship application after application, and even though she wasn't able to help me pay tuition, she never let me go hungry during those four years, or any of the years before. Earning that degree was as thrilling to her as it was to me. I really miss her now.

And I really miss my dad, this mostly absent ghost that lingered here and there through my childhood, and even less in my adulthood. I wonder how things would have been different if he were still alive. I wonder if he would have been as happy, standing next to mom and me in my cap and gown. My mind flashed back to that old picture I found in the box of my mom's things. It is the only picture I have of him that isn't completely packed away.

I rummage more through the box of my mom's things that I have come to accept will never be emptied and will probably travel with me as-is if I ever move out of this place. The picture is still where I left it, in the pocket of my mom or possibly my dad's sweatshirt, put there years and years ago.

The man is definitely my father. He is probably about my age there. The sun is shining, and it looks like a beautiful day. The boy, supposedly Alex, is beaming as he stands under the arm of my father. It is so odd to me that they look completely comfortable with each other, and even more odd that this boy seems vaguely familiar, though I can't place him in any of my memories. The yard they're standing on is lush and healthy, completing the picture-perfect scene of this mystery place behind them. The house has writing on it in fancy black script: "Four Hundred Sycamore". The address is unfamiliar, but the picture is strangely comforting to me. I don't have any family left and being able to hold on to this one tangible part of my father makes me feel less alone. I put the picture back in its aged envelope and wrap myself in the sweatshirt as I try to sleep through another quiet night.

6 Tiramisu, cheesecake, and chocolate mousse

The end of this work week brings excitement on Friday! Emily, Zanna, and I have a night out planned, but it is largely a mystery to me. Dinner, of course, is the first stop. They tell me to dress for fun and be ready at 7:30 when my Uber will be waiting. I have no idea where were are going, but I am so excited to get out and do something.

I take extra care in getting ready tonight since it is the first time in so long. Getting dressed up with a glass of bubbly in one hand is definitely a way to boost the mood. I find my favorite skinny jeans, stilettos, and a shinny grey tank top. My hair is done up and my earrings are dangling. At 7:30 sharp, my Uber driver arrives. The sleek black Audi Q5 only elevates my excitement for a posh night out. After driving for 15 minutes, we pull up to the best seafood restaurant in all of Utah. The chef is known statewide, and the view of the mountains from the entire wall of windows is breathtaking. I'm glad I have been saving a bit more with not going out much, because tonight will be a much needed splurge.

Zanna is waiting at the door, looking as stunning as ever in her turquoise cocktail dress. Emily pulls up shortly after, donned in perfectly fitting black pants and a very flattering fuchsia top. We run to each other, laughing like we are in high school, and start the evening with linked arms.

The swordfish special is incredible, resting atop risotto, summer squash, and mushrooms. Zanna and Emily each enjoy the sampler that is aptly described as "one of everything". As usual, champagne accompanies our ocean smorgasbord. Emily is thrilled to have a night away from wiping noses and being a short-order cook for her two little ones. Her husband, Derrick, is one of the good ones. She doesn't have to worry about her family at home for the night. Always the level-headed one, she is determined to let loose tonight. Zanna talks about how she hasn't had a full night's sleep in three years since her daughter was born. She, however, has not let this change in lifestyle affect her spunk and love for excitement.

With Zanna and Emily's conversations drifting from work to play to family and back, I find myself being a bystander without much to add. This does not last long, when they finally refuse to dominate the chatter and demand an update on my life. What interesting morsel of gossip can I add here? I wake up, go to work, come home, and sometimes add to the excitement with laundry or late-night night reruns from the late 1990s. (Note the sarcasm.)

They push, and I tell them about work while they yawn dramatically. But then I have it! There is one new and not terrible thing I that can tell them about, though I'm nervous about the eye rolls that may ensue when they think this, too, is snooze-worthy. I tell them with as much enthusiasm as I can muster, hoping they'll buy in. I describe my success story of unpacking, mostly, and how I found comfort in my mother's box. I describe the floral scent that lingers and the comforting memories my mother's belongings evoke. There is no jeering or eye-rolling. My friends are nothing if not loving.

I don't have the picture with me, but I have dwelled on it enough that I can describe it perfectly from memory. I tell them how my father looks and how it is a picture I've never seen, with a home and a boy I've never seen. The sun seems warm and the smiles, even warmer. I offer details on the unfamiliar handwriting on the back, describing what was clearly a happy and important day.

When I finish, I slink back slightly, realizing how crazy I must sound to have the only dinner topic of import to be a long-winded and detailed account of a picture from long ago. I hope my friends don't take this as the last straw and have me committed.

Of course I'm wrong. They take a beat to process all that I've described, and start with questions:
"Where do you think this was?" "Are there any landmarks in the picture, even blurry in the background?" "Who is the boy? A cousin? A neighbor?" "Why would your mom keep this?"

With relief and a little bit of shame for doubting the two who have never let me down, I dive in to their questions with unabashed curiosity. Of course, we have no answers and no leads, especially without the picture to painstakingly examine.

After a dessert of tiramisu, cheesecake, and chocolate mousse that as always were devoured from the middle of the table with no particular owner, Zanna and Emily inform me that the night is still young. Our Uber picks us up, slightly less glamorous in a beat-up SUV, and takes us to part two.

The rest of the night involves loud music, some bad karaoke, and some even worse dancing between three different bars. We laugh and shout memories over the drum beats. The three of us shut the town down and get a ride back to my shanty, where we will stay for the night. Zanna and Emily's husbands, Cal and Derrick, send their love via FaceTime and promise to feed the children a wholesome breakfast in the morning. It will most definitely be donuts all around.

The next morning, I wake up to the most delicious, mouthwatering aroma that is the absolutely only thing I want to breathe in after a late night out. Emily has coffee brewing, three mismatched mugs at the ready, and an entire box of warm donuts just now delivered by the bakery down the street. The closing door must have been what woke me. It couldn't have been too loud though, because Zanna is still drooling on the edge of the bed where we crammed together last night.

"This must be what heaven smells like," I say as I give Emily the biggest hug I can manage with a mug in one hand and a sugary candied work of pastry art in the other. "If I had known donuts and coffee would bring this smile out of you, I would have been sending them to you every day for months," she smiles back at me. The thought conjures up images of Violet Beauregard, though slightly less blue.

Zanna all but crawls the three feet from the bedroom as she clutches her head. "Just coffee for you then!," Emily laughs and hands a steaming mug over. "Not so loud," Zanna croaks out, but all that does is cause Emily and me to erupt in laughter.

We only have about an hour together before my two favorites have to return to their adult lives of responsibility. Emily will be fine today. Zanna's fate for the day, on the other hand, is yet to be determined. We rehash the night and tell of our favorite parts. Mine is Zanna rapping with astonishing precision the entirety of Baby Got Back. Emily almost spits out her coffee when she remembers the three of us taking over the stage in an attempt to do the Backstreet's Back dance. It turns out we don't actually know the dance, nor should we.

As we start to wrap up, Emily brings up the picture. "Let's get dinner again this week to check it out and start some detective work. It may be nothing, but anything is better than dwelling on your ex-*what's his name*." "Yes!," says Zanna, "but this time let's sleep in our own beds at a more reasonable hour". We laugh, agree, and plan to talk soon. Once they're gone, the silence is noticeable but not despairing. I am still smiling with the leftover eyeliner smudges and lingering coffee smells reminding me that I am not really alone. I grab the picture and start to take notes. A new task is exactly what I need. I recite the questions asked last night, starting with where this picture could be taken and who this boy could be. The answers seem far away and unlikely to find, but I am drawn to this unknown.

7 My apparently haggard look

By noon, I have my list. I have painstakingly noted anything interesting in the picture, including the time of year (probably spring), the types of plants surrounding the yard (desert willows and possibly hydrangea), and the fact that there is an intersection visible in the picture's background. By searching the internet on my ever-so-slow laptop, I've made a list of possible cities where this particular Four Hundred Sycamore could be. Without knowing more, the list is long and includes Four Hundred Sycamore Roads, Drives, Ways, and so on. There are only ten or so options that I find in Utah though, which feels like I may have a little bit of a lead. Remembering our plans to work this out together, I put my pen and paper down and grab my phone.

How does dinner on Monday sound?, I tap out via text to Zanna and Emily. Zanna quickly replies that Monday evenings are reserved for grocery shopping with the family, but wonders if Thursday would work. We wait for Emily to respond, though it may be a while. She is not tied to her phone when she's at home with her family. She is probably in her backyard picking berries with Derrick and the kids or doing something equally as likely to be found in a fairy tale.

Inspired by what I envision Emily's day to be like, I change out of my sleep clothes, run a brush through my hair, and put on my sneakers and jacket. A walk and fresh air will do me some good. Leaving my phone on the table, I walk down the stairs and out into the cool, winter sunlight.

Some thirty minutes later, I return and see that I've missed several texts from my friends. Emily agrees to Thursday for dinner and then quickly worries that I have not responded immediately like usual. With fast thumbs, I reassure them both that I am ok as we outline our plans for Thursday.

The weekend continues in its usual drowsy way. I wake up, exist, and go to sleep. When Monday morning comes, I'm ready to start moving and get to work. I only have four work days to get through until my dinner out. I get to the office early, log in, and open my email. There are the usual daily news blasts, birthday announcements, and a few routine notes from clients following up on orders. There is one new email from my boss titled, "Let's talk". My stomach churns as I comb through my memory of the past few weeks. Have I been too distant? Are my skills slipping? A little shaky, I click open the message to find with no relief, that my boss, Marsha, wants to meet with me at 2:00 this afternoon in person.

I wish the email would have come later in the day, because I can't tear my mind away from it. Even so, I answer emails and make phone calls as usual and find myself able to secure a few more sales to current clients. During my lunch break, I nibble on my sandwich and do my best to make small talk with my co-workers. The pit in my stomach does anything but fade. Finally, 2:00 comes around, and I gather my courage. I have never been called to an in-person meeting without knowing why before, and even those for which I could prepare have been few. This job is steady and does not require a ton of micromanagement, so most of us are left to work on our own. I tap lightly on Marsha's door, and she asks me to close it before taking a seat. Her oversized windows allow the sunshine to pour in. She makes brief pleasantries and asks how I've been doing, and I respond by asking about her family in turn. With no more preamble, Marsha stands from her chair and begins to pace with her hands clasped behind her back. Her beige pant suit seems more formal than I'm used to. It's typically pretty laid back here, and this is adding to my stress.

"I'm not sure if you are aware, Lydia, but sales are not what they used to be here," Marsha jumps into it. I gulp and assure her that my numbers have been stable, if not slowly climbing. As if I've said nothing, she continues. "Upper management is taking a closer look at our staff and our productivity, and budget season is upon us. We are being forced to make hard decisions, one of the parts of this job that I find the most challenging."

My mind swirls. What am I going to do? I lost my mother and my marriage already. How can I also lose my job? I need this job to stay afloat, both financially and for my sanity. Marsha must see the panic in my eyes and in the white-knuckled grip I have on the arms of one of her ornate office chairs. She softens and quickly adds, "No, Lydia, you are doing very well. I'm sorry to have scared you. Beverly, however, has had consistently low numbers."

"Thank you for noticing my efforts," I say as I try not to make my relief too obvious. I have just been going through the motions recently. I am so grateful to know that this has been enough. "I'm sorry to hear about Beverly though. I'd be happy to work with her if you think that would help. I can even make some time today..."

"Actually, I have a different way for you to help," Marsha cuts me off. "I'd like you to work with Beverly to learn about her clients. Work with her for the rest of today and all of tomorrow to learn as much as you can. I'd like this transition to be as easy as possible for her customers." There is a brief, but palpable pause. "What are you saying?," I ask nervously. "I will have a talk with Beverly on Wednesday at the end of the day. Don't worry. There will be a nice severance package. She will be compensated for her time with us here."

"Marsha, I appreciate you letting me know all of this, but I'm a little uncomfortable. I would be lying to Beverly." The concern is obvious in my wavering inflection. Marsha butts in again before I can say more. "This is a good opportunity for you, Lydia. You will be able to get overtime, grow your numbers, and work your way up. You will be helping the company by picking up the slack."

I leave Marsha's office a little unsure of what just happened. I go directly to the restroom to gather myself. I rationalize by thinking Beverly will be let go regardless of how I handle this. If I react poorly, I will probably be let go too. Besides, Marsha said she will be given a severance package, right? This is beyond my control and it would be irresponsible of me to not take this as an opportunity. I take a few deep breaths, plaster on a smile that I hope looks genuine, and walk up to Beverly.

I immediately notice pictures of Beverly's family on her desk. She has two teenage boys, at least they were teenagers when the picture was taken, who look very similar to her husband, displayed on the opposite end of her desk. I try my best to be vague but truthful, and I tell her that Marsha wants me to help her with some of her clients. She smiles gratefully and accepts the help to get caught up, as she admits to falling behind lately. I feel my smile waver and the knot in my stomach twist. Luckily, we only have part of the afternoon to work together. By the end of the work day, I can barely gather my things fast enough to flee what I can only describe as a crime scene.

I need to think this through, and I wish I could call my mother. I know that I can't, so I immediately change into my gym clothes and dash back out into the winter air, hoping there is no small talk surrounding my elliptical today. My music and headphones are cued up to take me through the next half hour in hopes of sorting through all that is swirling in my head.

The rhythm of the movement helps me to think. I'm uncomfortable with deceiving Beverly, but I finally accept that this is a determination made at management levels above me. I am about as able to change the decision as I am able to to run the entire company, so it makes the most sense to embrace this as an opportunity. I am compelled to remember that this is business and not personal. I wipe the sweat from my forehead and bundle up for my short walk home.

Wednesday is filled with the same awkwardness for me. At about 4:00, Beverly is called into Marsha's office. I feel terrible and guilt ridden, though I know this is not my doing. After 15 minutes, I flee to the restroom and find myself once again trying to compose myself. I pace, wash my hands twice, brush my hair, and accept that I have nothing else to reasonably do in here. I gather my courage and walk back to Beverly's desk where we had been working together. She is already there with tears in her eyes. My stomach clenches, and I feel nauseated. "I'm so sorry, Beverly," I manage to say as I watch her pack the pictures of her sons and husband from her desk. She looks at me with barely veiled suspicion and asks to be left alone. "Of course." I will be such a hypocrite if I try to help. I hide in my cubical and do my best to look busy for the rest of the day before I put my head down and leave, purposely staying a few minutes after everyone else.

That night, I reassure myself that tomorrow will be a new, promising day at work. I am able to busy myself with preparations for dinner with Zanna and Emily. I text a few restaurant options, and we decide on a Mexican mainstay down the road from Zanna's house. Taco *Thursday* sounds like an excellent decision. I prep a bag for tomorrow with a change of clothes and make up to freshen up, and I set out the picture of my father with my notes. After I'm showered and in my PJs, I wrap up in my mother's cream sweater and look at the picture.

With renewed energy, I use my phone to search for information about my father again. There is nothing different. I'm not sure what I expected, but this lack of any information at all is frustrating. With my mom gone and no other family to talk with, internet searching is all that I have to find answers. I sigh and hope my friends will have a stroke of innovation and luck tomorrow. I crawl into bed, actually tired and not dreading the night ahead.

When it is finally Thursday morning, I leave the apartment for work with an odd combination of calm and shame. I am relieved to work without Beverly today, but I cannot stop envisioning those tears in her eyes as she gathered the pictures of her family. I hope that her husband has a good job and maybe that her sons are old enough by now to already be working themselves. I cannot imagine trying to raise a family while unemployed.

I barely have time to dwell on this once I'm at my desk, because I am immediately shocked to see 45 unread emails in my inbox. I scroll through and realize everything that Beverly was working on has unceremoniously been forwarded to me. I swallow the anxiety bubbling up in my gut and dive head first into the messages. Between these emails, the ones that follow throughout the day, and the unrelenting phone calls, I barely notice my coworkers drifting out in the evening. I never even finished my lunch! I hammer out the last few notes of the day, and realize I must head straight to dinner without changing unless I want to be late. I do not want to be the one to stand between Emily and her tacos.

I rush in to the restaurant only five minutes late, and the first comment is on my apparently haggard look. I give them the rundown of my week while my eyes pour over the margarita specials. Emily and Zanna are sympathetic about the position I was put in and hope that gaining clients will be worth it. They assure me that it will get easier once I get my bearings. We all hope there are no more cuts at work, and especially none where I am involved.

Zanna and Emily fill me in on their lives. We order a sampler of beef, chicken, fish, and veggie tacos with nachos and a pitcher of margaritas. Emily nearly bites the waiter's hand in her haste to eat. Soon, our stomachs are getting full and work is forgotten. We are laughing like always. I am not able to wait any longer, so I pull the reason for the evening out of my bag for my friends to inspect. I add my handwritten list of notes to the table, and Emily sets her shiny new tablet next to it while the three of us crowd around one half of the small, oval table.

Zanna commandeers the tablet and dives in by searching "Alex Burke 1985," "Alex Burke 1978," and "Gregory and Alex Burke, Utah". I almost choke on my nachos. "You think this kid is my older brother?!" Zanna shrugs, "It would be the easiest explanation. Occam's Razor and all that." "My mother would have told me if I had a brother," I snap. "Sorry! I wasn't trying to offend you. I just thought it would be a great start to rule it in or out right off the bat." "It is now effectively ruled out," I say, with my heart beating more rapidly than I'd like to admit. I am surprised to realize there was a part of me that wondered this. This so-called Alex has blonde curls like my dad and me, but his blue eyes and slender nose are not ours.

Emily jumps in by taking my list of "Four Hundred Sycamore" addresses, and she begins to search for street views. Her change of focus helps me to breathe a little easier, and Zanna orders another pitcher. I add a round of waters to the request while Zanna smirks. We talk about the upgrades a house would likely have had in 30 years, including new paint, a fence, a change in landscaping, and even additions to the footprint.

By the end of the night, we have solidly ruled out several locations and hypotheses. We are all hooked, though, and there is no going back. We split a to-do list comprised of online profile stalking, résumé searches, and street views of possible picture locales. We hug goodbye, and Emily whispers in my ear that she is proud of me for not even seeming to *think* of Jared tonight. I realize that it is true and squeeze her harder. I am more motivated than ever to tackle this new task and crack the mystery of Gregory and Alex.

8 The SLC Times

Friday went by in a similar blur. The day was crammed with tasks from my role as well as Beverly's. Now at the end of the day, I try to remind myself that this is supposed to be a compliment, a testament to my abilities and work ethic. Somehow, it feels like a punishment instead. I have no plans tonight, so I stay an extra hour or so in the now-dim office, catching up after everyone is gone. I realize I am working two jobs now, but hope it will calm down once I can find a system that keeps me efficient. The extra hours tonight will be a nice addition to my paycheck deposit.

Exhausted, I trudge home in the dark. The snow is howling, and I have to wrap my scarf around my face so that only my eyes are visible. My breath warms my face against the wool, but it isn't enough to stop me from shivering. By the time I make it home, there are snowflakes covering me top to bottom. I order pizza delivery from my phone and turn on the hot water in the shower.

The steam feels comforting, and the cloudiness in the bathroom allows my thoughts to stay hidden almost as well as my surroundings.

Before long, I hear the doorbell and curse. I was so far out of it that I forgot how hungry I was. I throw on a towel and drip a trail of water from my shower ledge to the apartment door. Keeping my body hidden as much as possible behind the door, I throw cash into the delivery person's hand before slamming the door, possibly too aggressively.

I collapse on the couch and eat straight from the box. The rest of the night is spent watching old television until it is late enough to try to sleep. The exhaustion from the busy day allows me to sleep again, and I am grateful.

Tuesday and Wednesday are repeats of Monday. I am getting used to my new routine, though this means I am getting comfortable staying late, alone at the office. I remind myself that the paycheck will be worth it. By Thursday night, I realize I have barely talked with Zanna or Emily all week. I flip through my phone and see the texts that were hurriedly read and replied to earlier. I take a minute to let them know I am alive and ok, but that I have been busy at work. They share condolences for my accruing hours and ask how my research is going. Emily thinks she has a few leads on where the picture may have been taken. Zanna says that she found some professional profiles and résumés that we should check out. I am ashamed to have nothing to add. My friends, of course, assure me that it is ok before asking if I am free Saturday night. There is nowhere I would rather be than with them. I promise to be prepared by Saturday before I grab my laptop and let it slowly start up. The microwave warms a frozen meal while I wait.

Tonight, I take a different approach to searching. I start with the address from the picture along with some details of my father. One story from 1987 catches my eye. A short newspaper clipping outlines an alarming court case. A man named Gregory was charged in the murder of an underaged boy. The location says Salt Lake City, and my heart stops. The webpage has the preview from a newspaper of long ago, but the full article is not included. I find the name of the newspaper, *SLC Times*, and start digging.

The newspaper did not have electronic editions in the '80s, and scanned files are only available back through the early 2000s. Instead of setting this aside and searching for any other information I can find, I can't help but focus on where and how I can get older copies of the SLC Times. I haven't been to a library in ages, and I'm not even sure how searching old newspapers works. This new discovery takes me down a rabbit hole where I bounce between library websites and online "how-tos". Before I know it, it's after 2:00 in the morning. A different wave of panic rushes over me. I do my best to calm down and get as much sleep as I can, but I know that this is unlikely tonight. I make a mental note to fill my extra large coffee mug in the morning.

Sooner than I would have liked, my alarm sounds. It isn't really necessary; I barely shut my eyes last night. Every time I did, a different and progressively more unlikely scene played behind my eyelids. I imagined my father in jail, on the run and living in the wilderness like a hobbit, murdered in prison by inmates, and on and on. No scenario is pleasant, though all seem unlikely in the light of the morning. Between the replay of each storyline from my dreams, I remind myself of what I knew about my father and feel ashamed. Before I know it, my imagination begins to run away again.

The ever-growing bags under my eyes underline the exhaustion that my body and mind feel. I know that today will be tough, so I grab an extra donut and fill my mug to the brim. My inbox is as full as ever, and I am once again glued to my desk for the next several hours. After lunch, Marsha stops by and not so subtly looks me up and down. She asks how I am enjoying the new opportunities for clients. I show as much enthusiasm and gratitude as I can muster while trying to ignore the *ping* that signals another email vying for my attention.

Marsha doesn't seemed too convinced, but she is out of my mind as soon as she walks away. I manage to leave only one hour late tonight. I know I could stay longer to start off in a good place on Monday, but I am completely exhausted. Before heading out, I remember to check my bank account and smile big when I see the extra funds from my overtime. I do some fast math and calculate what my next deposit might look like with more than two days of extra hours.

When I get home, I crash on the couch without dinner. My mind attempts to replay the scenes of my father from the night before. I drift in and out of sleep, trading imagination for nightmares. Eventually, my body gives up and I sleep until the sunlight from my living room window hits me square in the eyes.

I wince, stretch, and vow to buy a new couch once I earn more overtime funds. My coffee pot calls to me. Most of the morning is spent nearly comatose on the couch, sipping coffee and reeling from the previous week's work intertwined with my latest find about my father. By noon, I finally feel able to focus, so I search the internet for newspapers with digital editions from 1987. I have no luck, but I am able to compile a list of libraries where I may be able to search archives.

My mind shifts to my mother. "Hazel Alecia" has a much different response online since her death was so recent. Her memorial page is the first result, and her picture stares back at me. I chose one of my favorite pictures of my mother to show her as she truly was: outside under a willow tree, surrounded by freshly cut grass, looking pure with almost no make up. The sun is shining and there is a book in her hand. I took this picture when we met for lunch one day so long ago.

My heart hurts to see her face again. I wish I would have asked her more about my father. I wish I would have asked her advice about my marriage. Really, I just wish I could hear her voice again.

Rather than allow myself to spiral, I decide to lace up my shoes and go for a walk. Sure, it's winter in Utah, but at least it isn't sleeting. I layer up with my warmest alpaca mittens, a scarf, and my fur-lined trapper hat. My breath is visible as soon as I hit the sidewalk, which is speckled with newly scattered rock salt. I know I won't be out for long, but I'm glad to be moving. I'm reminded that I spent last night on the couch, because my first few steps are stiff. The movement and fresh air helps to ground me, and by the time I make it around a few blocks, I'm shivering but feeling ready for the night ahead.

The hot shower feels wonderful after the cold air, and I mentally pick out which sweater and boots I'll wear to dinner tonight. I remember that I've barely eaten anything today, and my mouth starts to water as if on cue. Once I'm out of the shower, I check my phone and am excited to see that Zanna suggested a local downtown restaurant for tonight. The barbecue chicken is to die for there. An hour later, I'm hopping out of my Uber and into the cacophony of happy eaters and the smell of a Deep South kitchen. My friends wave from across the restaurant, and I nearly run to them, fueled by my need to spill all that I have learned in my online research.

We barely say hello before I blurt out, "I think my dad may have been a murderer." The silence from Emily and Zanna is louder that the mass of patrons surrounding us. Zanna is the first to talk. "No. That can't be right," she says slowly. I fill them in on the newspaper clipping I found while pulling it up on my phone. They read the snip-it about four times each. Zanna finally blurts out, "Well, that's pretty damning."

Emily rolls her eyes and all but pushes Zanna out of her chair. "It is not," she says forcefully. "That is an incredibly small paragraph that doesn't even have a last name listed. It could be so many other people."

"But Emily," Zanna nearly yells, "this makes total sense! Why can't we find anything, even an obituary, on Gregory. The internet has everything and then some, but no death notice? That does not happen. This explains why Hazel barely talked about Lydia's father, too. Who would want their child to know their father is rotting in jail for the worst of all crimes? Hazel would absolutely try to shield Lydia."

Emily responds, "You are wrong. We knew Hazel. She wouldn't have married a murderer, and she definitely wouldn't have kept something like this from Lydia. How can you even think such a thing!"

Zanna starts to argue her point further when I mumble, "But they weren't married." The two take a minute to process this, because it was barely audible. I also think they forgot that I was there for a bit between their bickering. "My parents, Hazel and Gregory. They weren't married," I say louder, possibly too loud this time. The couple in the adjacent booth quiet and glance over at me.

I drop my voice and build off of Zanna's theory. "This has to be it. My father is alive in prison for the murder of a child, and my whole life has been a lie." At the worst possible time, the waitress finally arrives to take our drink orders. The discomfort is palpable for only a second before Emily takes charge and orders an entire bottle of Pinot Grigio with three glasses. This conversation is going to need some liquid courage.

The second the waitress is gone, three phones and six quick thumbs comb the internet for anything that may have been overlooked. By the time our glasses are filled, we agree that we need to investigate actual newspapers from 1986 and 1987 to find the full story. We each take an aggressively long gulp from our glasses and refocus our search. Over dinner, we devise a plan and schedule from the list of libraries I've organized. Emily reminds us of her research training while in college, but quickly clarifies that she only took the two required courses when she sees our raised eyebrows. It may not be a Ph.D. in Criminal Justice, but it's the best we've got.

Thankfully, we are all free tomorrow. Zanna and Emily confirm with their husbands that they won't be missing anything for two hours in the afternoon. We plan to meet at the nearest library on our list at noon sharp. Zanna will bring the coffees, Emily will be ready to lead the detective work, and I just hope that I can keep it together.

9 HelpYouHelpMe

Winter in Utah can be brutal. Last night, it snowed eight inches. Most drivers here are well-versed in winter driving, but this much powder at one time is enough to slow anyone down. When I looked out my window this morning, my heart sank when I thought our sleuth plans for the day would be derailed. My concern with the snow on top of my already fried nerves about today caused me to find myself ready almost two hours early. I have the time, so I decide to strap on my snow boots and walk to the library. It will be easier than driving or getting a ride for a little while anyhow. Ten minutes into my walk, my stomach knots. I am nervous, but I also have reverted back to my poor eating habits since my job has become so much more demanding. I have also stayed away from the gym for too long. It's obvious my body's aches are from more than just anxiety today.

The warmth of the library greets me. I stomp the snow off of my boots and peel off my layers. There are signs for private study rooms and most are empty, probably because of the snow. I choose the first room and set up camp, my pile of outerwear making the room look lived in immediately. There are two computers in the room, and I start both of them up. One has an extra large screen designed for viewing old documents in the library files, including 30 year old newspapers.

It takes me a while to find archives, sort by media form, and then finally sort by newspaper title. I double click on *SLC Times* right as the door to my study room clicks open. Emily is here to join me, a full half hour early. She has a coffee in each hand, knowing she will be early, Zanna will be late, and there's a pretty good chance Zanna will forget coffee. Grateful, I hug her and grab my coffee in the same motion. I fill her in on the very little bit of progress I've made. We look at hundreds of newspaper choices on the screen. Finding 1987 is blessedly easy, but scanning though all pages of each edition is tedious.

It takes about 20 minutes to find the teaser court article that we saw online. Zanna arrives to our room, surprising us at a few minutes before noon. She looks windswept and is still stomping snow off of her boots. We are pleased to have her join us, but slightly disappointed to see that her hands are empty. Seeing our two coffees, she grimaces and apologizes. "I'll run across to Jake's Café for refills when we need it." Jake's is a cozy place for brunch, and it has been forever since I've been there. It wasn't open when I walked past on my way in. If it does open up despite the snow, it will be a great place for a bite to eat too. I know we're going to need it.

Emily tells Zanna what we've found so far as I skim the pages. The black, white, and grey are making my eyes blur. On the front page of the legal section, the title "Utah man charged in brutal murder of young neighbor" stands out as if in neon lights. "Guys," I say nervously. They are immediately crouched over me as I shakily scroll down. The picture starts out grainy and takes a few extra seconds to load while we read the words around it. The article begins with a detailed account of how the verdict was delivered. The presiding juror was dramatic in his announcement. When asked what the jury found, he paused long enough to scan the courtroom and then lock eyes with the defendant before bellowing, "guilty".

The picture finishes loading, and our eyes dart over. Zanna and Emily don't say anything, and I swallow hard. The picture shows a disheveled defendant attempting to look proper in a plaid suit and tie. The man is not my father.

The room is silent for several minutes. I hear my heartbeat. The edges of my vision blur, and I feel sick. Emily's light touch on my arm brings me back. "Is this good news or bad news?," she asks me gently. It takes only a second to find my voice. "It's good news. Definitely good news." I take a gulp of air and start to relax. My feelings are a mix of immense relief, terrible guilt, and a touch of regret with frustration.

We talk for a bit and process out loud to each other. We all seem to have similar mixes of emotion. Of course this is good news, but what next? What happened in my father's past? Having found an answer of any type, even if terrible, might be better than just more questions.

Zanna startles us by jumping to her phone. "I found something last night that I wasn't sure would be helpful. Now that we are back at square one, check this out. There's this forum called *HelpYouHelpMe*. I've been looking into it to make sure it isn't a scam or anything, and it seems pretty legit. People post anything and everything to see if anyone can help find answers. There are people on here asking for help with physics homework, getting tips on how to cook the perfect Thanksgiving turkey, and all kinds of things *including* finding lost loved ones. They even have a few employed researchers to make sure the harder questions have a shot at getting answered. It might be worth a try." She shrugs and looks nervous.

Emily and I each take a computer while Zanna continues on her phone. We follow separate threads and talk out loud and over top of each other about the stories. Some mysteries go unsolved, but all have some type of response. When we read the happy ending of an adopted child reuniting with her birth mother, we decide it's time to create an account.

We click on a section aptly named "People Finder". There is a disclaimer saying that some people do not want to be found, and that any suspicious or unsavory activity will be shared with authorities. We start a post and title it simply, "Daughter Looking for Father". We upload a copy of the picture and give only a few details. We ask for clues on where the picture was taken, though we suspect northern Utah. We ask if there is any information on Gregory Burke or the child, possibly named Alex. We hit save, but not post. I need to be sure this is the right move.

We decide to stretch our legs and fill our stomachs by walking to Jake's. The amount of time it takes to bundle up makes us second guess ourselves, but then Zanna's stomach rumbles loudly. We laugh and keep layering.

Jake's is thankfully open and invitingly warm. We grab a table in the corner, order sandwiches, and sit back to relax and enjoy the soft coffee house music playing overhead. There are only a few people here. Most are probably staying home because of the snow, though it looks like the roads have mostly been cleared in the time we were in the library. My stomach has been tied in knots, but when our sandwiches arrive, the smell helps me to get past any lingering nausea.

Zanna and Emily want to get back to their families rather than return to the library, so when we finish eating, Zanna pulls up our pending post. We read and re-read it, and then collectively decide to hit submit. My nausea is instantly back, and I pray that we did not open a can of worms or invade anyone's privacy but my own. My friends assure me that this will be ok, and more importantly, that they are doing this with me. We hug, start the process of layering up again, and say our goodbyes.

My walk home allows me to think. I do my best thinking when I'm moving, and it feels soothing to be able to do this again. I have been so busy at work and so unmotivated before that, that my thoughts and feelings have built up. I decide to go just a little past my apartment building before heading home. I run through the past days, weeks, and then months. The pain in my heart for both Jared and my mother spikes for a minute, then lessens to a manageable twinge that may always be present for me.

Once back at my apartment, I collapse onto my couch in an exhaustion that feels both physical and emotional. The rest of the day is filled with lounging and sweatpants. Eventually I convince myself to cook dinner, something that I have not done in many days. I eat with the television on and fiddle through my phone.

My mind won't shut off, so I pile on the outerwear once again and make my way to the gym in the dark evening of winter. The bright lights inside surprise me. With my headphones on, I start on the elliptical. An hour has gone by before I know it, and my body suddenly feels heavy. I barely remember my workout and have no clue what songs were playing. I wonder what my face looked like, because I was completely zoned out.

When I'm home, showered, and laying down in bed, I pray for the sleep that my body craves. I will myself not to look at my phone, but rather to start counting sheep. Somewhere around 2:00am or 1000 sheep, I drift into uneasy sleep.

My eyes burn when I open them. I know it's early by the dim sunlight trying to peak around my blinds. My mind goes directly to *HelpYouHelpMe*. Before sitting up, before even wiping the sleep from my tired eyes, I grab my phone and log in. There is a new message titled, "Sycamore". I think my heart completely stops beating, and I am no longer breathing. The message says simply:

"I know this house. Who are you?".

10 Strong, reliable women

I stare at my phone for a long time. I'm not sure if this is real or if it is someone scamming me. I need to find out more, but I also need to be smart about it. I take a screen shot and send it to Zanna and Emily. Zanna's immediate response makes me laugh a little, as if she was staring at her phone dying for an update. It says only, "*Woah*". A few seconds later, she adds, "*What are you going to say?*". Emily is not far behind and warns me to be careful and to not share more than is necessary.

I put my phone down so I don't react to the Sycamore message irrationally. I press the start button on the coffee instead. Standing in my kitchen, I rub my eyes and try to wake up and think things through. I listen to the *drip drip* of coffee and smell the comforting morning aroma. Once my mug is full, I breathe in the scent, grab my phone, and take a seat at my table.

I type and delete three drafts before deciding what to send. My message eventually says:

This is a picture of my father, but I'm not sure who the boy is.
My dad is dead. I want to know more about him.
How do you know this house?

It's short, direct, and not overly descriptive. I hope it's enough. I want this person to answer me, but I do not want to share too much. I think of a carnival fortune teller and need to know that anything this stranger tells me is not created from information I accidentally give.

I figure it's time to start my day, so I list the things I need to do:
-Grocery shop
-Do some type of physical activity
-Get ready for the work week
-Maybe clean my apartment

That's it. I take about five seconds to try to decide what to do next, but before I get too far, I hear *ping* from my phone. *Zanna and Emily must be checking in*, I think to myself. But no. It is a notification from the website. The responder has already answered me back.

Where do you live? Can we meet for coffee near Ogden?

I can't believe this person wants to meet without talking more. Ogden isn't terribly far. I could meet him or her, but is this safe? What would they say? Why wouldn't they just send an email. Something feels off, and I know I can't meet them. Not yet.

I respond back:
I'm not able to meet right now. Can we talk over email or text?

The stranger quickly answer that text is ok and sends a phone number. I'm very surprised that they are willing to share this so easily. I immediately search the number online for any identifying information. The number is definitely a northern Utah phone number, and the service provider is listed, but there is no name or anything else to go off of. I want to take a minute to think about what to do. I should call or text Zanna and Emily and maybe even meet *them* for coffee to decide how to handle this. I know I can't wait though. I need answers now.

I type out the digits and start and re-start several messages. Finally, I type only *Hi. This is Lydia.* The text bubbles pop up in a matter of a few seconds, showing that this mystery person is replying already. It takes a while, and the bubbles start and stop a few times. They are having trouble finding what to say, just like I did. Finally, the conversation starts.

Them: *Hi Lydia. Where did you get this picture?*
Me: *I found it in my dad's old things.* It's a little bit of a lie, but there's no need to share too much right now.
Them: *I used to live on that street. I moved away about 12 years ago.*
Me: *Did you know my dad? What about the boy?*
Them: *Maybe. Why do you think your dad saved this? What is your dad's name?*
I'm starting to feel uneasy. Me: *I'm not sure. His name was Greg.*

The bubbles stop. No more texts come.

Me: *Hello?*
Nothing.

Me: *Did you know him?*
Nothing.

How strange for this person to stop talking. They must have known my dad! Another part of my brain tells me that they may have a good reason for not responding. Not everyone is glued to their phone, and maybe he or she is in the middle of something important. Maybe they have a family who needs attention. Maybe they are at work. It still feels like odd timing to just stop talking.

A half hour goes by with no response. I am too nervous to keep texting, at least for now, because I don't want to scare my only lead off forever. I decide that now is the perfect time to start my chore list for the day, so I silence my phone to see if it helps to silence my thoughts.

Hours later, all of my tasks are crossed off of my list. I un-silence my phone, and my heart sinks a little when I see that there are no messages from the mystery person. I do, however, have several missed text messages from Zanna and Emily. They want to know what I am thinking, feeling, and doing. They ask if I replied to the person from *HelpYouHelpMe*. They ask where I am and why I'm not responding. They ask if I'm ok.

I am lucky to have these strong, reliable women in my life. I take a deep breath and relay all that has happened. Still, there is no more response from the mystery person. My friends respond quickly and only slightly chastise me for being MIA all day. *I'm sorry. I needed some time to think,* I type back to them. They understand, as they always do, and ask me how I'm feeling. We talk for a while, and my nerves calm. I know that even if I never hear back from this person, I will be ok.

But still.

There's still a catch in my breathing and a lull in my heartbeat. I pray for answers. For reconciliation. For peace. But this will not happen tonight, I know. Instead, I ensure everything is ready for work tomorrow, and I climb into bed. I hope I can sleep tonight.

11 No offense, Lydia

It's the start of another work week, and winter is rearing its head. The snow is falling again, and the dull grey light trying to shine through the windows does not let me forget that it is Monday. I have more emails than ever, and the message light is flashing on my phone. I am overwhelmed before I even sit down. I dive in and type, working as fast as I possibly can. Before I know it, my stomach growls, announcing that it is time for lunch. The email notification number keeps climbing, and I decide to eat quickly in front of my computer with one hand still on the keyboard.

My shoulders ache and my eyes are tired. There is a subtle pain in the back of my head that tells me I have barely moved or taken my eyes away from the screen in several hours. "Hey Lydia," a coworker named Courtney says quietly. I gasp in surprise, completely oblivious of my surroundings. "Hi Courtney. I'm sorry, I've been drowning in work. I didn't even notice you come over."

"You've been glued to your desk for a few weeks now. Is it because you have all of Beverly's work plus your own?," she asks.

"Yes. I'm happy for the opportunity and for the overtime, but it's a lot." I try to ignore the flashing voicemail light on my desk phone and take a deep breath.

"Marsha had me shadow Michael last Thursday and Friday. Now he's gone, and I have his entire job on top of mine. I know it's only my first day with this, but it is too much. How are you handling this all?"

My silent look at Courtney along with the shadows growing under my eyes are the only answers she needs. "That's what I was afraid of. Do you have time to grab a drink after work?," Courtney asks.

"I would love a cocktail. Meet me in the break room at 5:00?," I answer. My phone starts to ring, so I add, "Make that 6:00." Courtney frowns and trudges back to her desk.

By 5:30, I'm relieved to see that I have completed all of my supply orders, and my numbers are significantly higher than ever before. I mentally run through my new list of clients and realize there are two or three I haven't connected with in the past few days. I need to get organized so I don't fall behind. I decide to prioritize making a few lists and schedules for myself. I start with a list of current clients and then one of potential new clients. The lists are long and take time; making a schedule will have to wait until the morning. Instead, I make yet another list of the supplies I will need to complete a new organizational system. At a little after 6:00, I don't feel any better. There are still so many unchecked boxes on my mental to-do list.

I get to the break room only a few minutes late, but I see that Courtney is still at her desk. I can tell from here that she is frantically trying to find a place to stop. I should go back to my desk and work until Courtney is done, but my mind is fried. Instead, I check my phone for the first time all day. Zanna and Emily sent a few messages back and forth. They know by now that I rarely answer when I'm at work.

Below our group chat is a text adding to yesterday's thread from my new could-be informant.
I'm sorry I didn't answer your text before. I went for a hike.

He or she still didn't answer my question. This is confusing. Why text me at all if there is no information to share. I deliberate and decide to play it cool. *How was the hike?* I immediately feel ridiculous for trying to make small talk with this stranger. I'm thankful to see Courtney walking over, so I put my phone back on silent and try to put it out of my mind.

Courtney and I have never talked outside of work, so I'm a little nervous that this will be awkward. We warm up in the restaurant, and I order a margarita. She asks for a martini. Before long, we are both a little less on edge. Courtney looks around to see if anyone else from work is near us, but there is no sign of anyone we know. I'm not sure that the secrecy is necessary, and it strikes me as little silly. She leans in and asks how things are going for me at work. I tell her about my endless tasks, but that the extra money in my paycheck has been nice. It will be even nicer this Friday when I will have two full weeks with overtime every day.

Courtney is quiet but nods her head. I allow the silence just for a minute and then ask how she is doing. She agrees that the overtime pay will be great, but adds that she is very worried. She fills me in on some of the updates throughout the office that I missed while my head has been buried in my computer. I was the first one to take on an extra job: Beverly's. Then Charles took over Melissa's role. Now Courtney has taken over Michael's.

"I didn't realize three people have been fired. And so quickly! So the company is trying to keep up the same amount of work with half of the people? We can't possibly manage that!," I say, truly alarmed.

Courtney answers, "Paying us overtime makes it looks like they are helping us, but overtime costs much less than a full time person with benefits. They are only helping themselves. Anthony told me he is supposed to start working with Bruce by the end of the week, so you know what that means for Bruce. We can't do this forever. Charles is exhausted, today was rough for me, and no offense Lydia, but you look like you haven't slept in weeks."

"I haven't, but there's more to that than work," I tell her without elaborating.

"Oh. Right," she says. "I'm sorry." After a respectful pause, she adds, "But still, this amount of work is not sustainable. Charles and I think we should organize the rest of the team and talk with Marsha. Maybe she doesn't know how stretched thin we are becoming."

I hesitate. Courtney is right that we can't keep it up at this clip, but is it already time to make a scene like this? If the company is making cuts, we are among the lucky ones who still have jobs. I can't lose my only source of income. Courtney reads my face and asks what I'm thinking. I share my thoughts and worries. She tells me that she is nervous too and also relies on her sole paycheck. She is planning to redo her résumé this week and will send it to a few places, just in case.

This makes me panic. I didn't realize it was so serious! I thank her for filling me in, and we make a plan to talk with some of our co-workers throughout the week. I make a mental note to work on my résumé when I get home. It hasn't been updated for years, and I'm afraid no one would want to hire me. Where would I go? I finish my drink and try to calm down. We pay the tab and head out into the cold night, where we say our goodbyes and part ways. It was nice being with someone else rather than home alone on a week night. I feel guilty that I have never really talked with Courtney much. Now I wonder how many more chances I'll have.

At home, I'm surprised to see another message from the *HelpYouHelpMe* person. It says, *The hike was great! Thanks for asking. I went with a few of my buddies. It was very cold, but the scenery made it worth it.*

"Buddies." This must be a man talking with me. Refueled by the camaraderie of the evening out with Courtney, I decide to keep the conversation going. I have a few minutes to kill while my laptop slowly starts up anyhow. We send a few messages back and forth, thankfully not waiting hours in between each text like before. The conversation flows more smoothly than I expected. I learn that this man is adventurous and seems to have a large group of similar friends. He worked today, though I'm not sure in what field. I shared that I like to hike too (This is a bit of a stretch. It has probably been two years since the last time I hiked), and that I had a rough day at work. We share only a few details, but the exchange is easy.

Soon, we have been chatting for about an hour while I multitasked and finished a first draft of my new résumé. The idea of needing to use it makes me uncomfortable. I look at the clock and wince. I've done it again. Tomorrow will be another brutal day for several reasons, one of which will definitely be fatigue. I tell my new friend (is this what I should call him?) that I need to get to bed. He says he will talk to me soon. *What information can I get him to share with me tomorrow?,* I wonder.

12 On repeat

Other than the bright sunshine replacing the dreary skies, today is a repeat of yesterday. Charles gives me a few knowing looks, but there's no time to talk. We all work quietly and rush through our day. By Wednesday, I'm already burnt out. I stayed late yesterday and started early today. My numbers are excellent and continue to climb, so I keep telling myself that my paycheck will make this all worth it. I make a mental note to start comparing new laptops online.

Marsha walks over to my desk, stays silent until I finally look up and notice her, and then apologizes when I startle. She asks if I have a minute to grab some coffee. I absolutely do not have a minute, but I know that this is more of a rhetorical question. I agree and hope there was no noticeable hesitation in my response. She already has her coat in her hands. Marsha does not mean to have coffee and chat in the break room.

I feel pretty confident that Marsha wouldn't take someone away from the office just to fire them. I am curious, but cautious. Courtney eyes me on the way out, and Charles does his best not to stare. Our office was very different just a few weeks ago. If there was drama, I didn't know of it. I barely knew everyone's names. How did we get here so quickly?

As soon as we are on the sidewalk and the doors behind us are tightly closed, Marsha asks how I'm liking the overtime pay. "It's very helpful, thank you. How are you?" I hope that my measly attempt at small talk is less embarrassing than it sounds to me. Her smile becomes more of a smirk before she says that she is managing. We talk about nothing more than weather and traffic on the thankfully short walk to the coffee shop. It is crowded at this time of day, and we wait in line long enough to feel even more uncomfortable. After what seems like ages, we have our drinks in hand and slide into a corner booth. The conversations around us are rushed. Almost everyone dons business outfits and barely manages to say full sentences to each other between texts, emails, and hushed phone calls.

"How is the office morale, Lydia?," Marsha asks. This catches me off guard a little, and then I mentally and quickly replay the past several days. Marsha has been hiding out in her office for almost all of the time she has been at work. She is usually there before me, stays into the evening after I leave, and rarely comes out in between. I wonder if she is avoiding everyone or just overworked. Her eyes are more tired than mine.

"Well," I start cautiously, "I have noticed a few more empty desks". "Yes," she answers. "The cut backs are unfortunate. Unfortunate, but necessary. We are lucky that there aren't more empty desks."

"Does this mean the cuts are over? Maybe we can start splitting the extra work then." I've said too much, too eagerly. She knows we are overworked. She knows we are unhappy and stressed. But she also knows there is more change to come. And now she knows that I know that, too.

"Marsha. What can I do?" This is the question she has been waiting for me to ask.

"The team looks up to you, Lydia." *No they don't. What makes her think that?*

I don't know how it happened, but something about keeping my head down and working hard must have been noticed throughout. I was the first to be asked to do extra. I was the one Courtney came to. But what can I do? Which side do I chose? "I need you to keep up the morale." Marsha's voice cuts into my thoughts like a knife, the edge in her voice almost painful. "I need you to lead your coworkers. Assure them that if they work hard enough, no more cuts will have to be made. I trust you Lydia, and this company needs you to help us stay afloat. Think of your co-workers. Their families."

Here I am again. Is this a compliment or am I just a Yes Man? Do I even have a choice? Could this be a chance to move up, get a promotion? At what cost?

Marsha takes my silence as agreement. "I knew I could count on you, Lydia. You are an important part of this company, and I will make sure our management knows this. I do need your word that you won't talk about our meeting today though. This needs to stay between you and me. The others need to think of you as their leader because you've earned it. Not because I'm involved. And of course, that is the truth!"

We finish our coffees mostly in silence and head back to the office. Courtney finds me less than five minutes after I get back. "Drinks tonight?" I'm not sure what to say. I can't tell her what our meeting was about, and that is definitely why she wants to meet. But I want to help my co-workers, too. I'm not ready to decide. "I can't tonight. I have plans. Raincheck?" "Sure," she says, and all but runs back to her desk to answer her ringing phone.

It is nearly impossible to concentrate for the rest of the afternoon. Charles and Courtney both make a point to stop at my desk to say hi. They have never done that before, so I know they are trying to find out what happened today. They want to solidify our alliance.

I am so far behind from my coffee break and because I haven't been able to focus since I got back. I know I'll be here late again tonight. I pull out my cell and see a text from my new friend. I nicknamed him Adam in my phone to make the messages that pop up seem less crazy. This might be more crazy than just having an unidentified number though. *How is your day?*

It is so friendly. So easy and simple. And it is coming from someone who doesn't even know me. I realize he is a stranger on the outside who might be able to give me perspective and advice. I tell him I am having a challenging day, and soon after, he asks if I want to talk about it. I do. I tell him I need to finish up at work and will text him later. He gives me a thumbs up.

I stay at work until after 7:00 and drag myself home in the darkness of winter. As soon as I make it into my kitchen, I grab my phone and text "Adam" to tell him that I am finally home. Only a few minutes go by when my phone vibrates. He comments on the late hour and asks what's going on. I tell him everything about work. He interjects here and there, but mostly just lets me get everything off of my chest. When I'm finished, he doesn't tell me what to do. He doesn't even pressure me to make a decision. He just lets me breathe and sort it out myself. Laying it out there all at once does seem to make me see it more clearly. I know that I need my job. This is business, and business can be cutthroat. This is my time to have something good, to grow and advance, and to not live paycheck to paycheck. I tell him this, and he says that if I think it's the right move, it must be the right move.

There is silence for several minutes, and I busy myself by getting my things ready for tomorrow. My weekdays are on repeat. I hope that sticking with this will be worth it and eventually less exhausting. My phone vibrates and the message catches me off guard.

Tell me about your dad.

I nearly break my phone from dropping it. This is the reason we are talking to each other, but the change in topic is so abrupt that I'm not sure how to react. I want to give him all of the information I know. More than that, I want him to give me all of the information he knows. I need to keep him talking. If he knows anything about my dad or the boy in the picture, I need to get it out of him before he decides to stop texting.

Against my better judgement, I start to share just a tiny bit of my story.

Me: *My dad died when I was 5. I don't remember a lot about him, but I have this picture.*
Him: *Why do you think the picture's important?*
Me: *I'm not sure that it is. But it was saved after all of these years. I've been going through a lot of changes lately, and it seems like I found it just now on purpose.*
Him: *Did you grow up near Sycamore?*
Me: *I don't know. What town is it in?*

After a few minutes, he finally answers, *It is Sycamore Road in Layton, Utah.*
I do a quick map search to confirm.

Me: *I grew up about an hour away. I don't think I've ever been there. I wonder what was so important that my dad would go there.*
Silence.
Me: *I don't have anyone else to ask. I just wish I knew more about him.*
Him: *Do you have other pictures of him?*

I'm not sure why this would matter. I'm also unsure of why he is being so hesitant. I think about it for a few minutes before answering. *Yes, but they are still packed away.*

Our conversation is slowing with longer and longer gaps between replies. I get ready for bed and try to distract myself from impatiently staring at the screen. It is late, and we both need to try for sleep. He responds, *I'd love to see them sometime. Let's talk more tomorrow.*

I crawl in bed and replay the conversation. When I finally drift to sleep, the dreams of my dad play on repeat.

13 Dark roast, black

I settle into my workspace early and aim to keep my head down. It doesn't work. Courtney brings me a coffee and tries for some small talk. After just a few comments about her new clients and about how she is ready for spring, she dives in.

"Where did you go with Marsha?," she asks, not so casually. I tell her that we went for coffee and volunteer that Marsha asked how we were all dealing with the cuts. I hope that if I offer some information, she won't press me for much more. "Did she say that there are going to be more cuts?," she asks with more than a bit of panic in her eyes. "She wouldn't tell me that, Courtney. She did say that we are all doing well with the extra work. I think it's being noticed, and we should hang tight for a little bit longer. I bet we'll start being able to spread the extra work around soon." "Did she say that? That we will be able to share the work with everyone who is left?," Courtney whispers, though loudly.

I look around and hope she catches my subtle suggestion to talk softer. Marsha's light is on in her office, but the slatted blinds are drawn. I'm pretty sure she isn't able to see out. If she can, I hope she thinks I'm following her directions. And I really think that I am.

Maybe I can find a way to work both sides. I can keep the peace with my co-workers, while also being an advocate to and for Marsha. Maybe this is what she wants, and when all of this is over, I'll be looked at favorably by my coworkers, Marsha, and her bosses.

"She didn't say that much directly, but I think that's what she means. I bet she'll be taking you and Charles out to coffee soon to have a similar talk." This is as close to a lie as I want to come. I really have no idea if this will happen. "And Anthony, too?," she says with obvious skepticism.

"Oh no." I look over to Bruce's desk. Courtney tells me that he cleared it out yesterday evening. Apparently he made a little bit of a scene, loudly announcing that he has been a loyal employee here for five years. My head was such a mess yesterday that I didn't even realize it. I am ashamed at how self-absorbed I can be.

We hear the *click* of Marsha's door opening. Courtney raises her eyebrows and darts back to her desk before Marsha sees. I get back to my work and tell myself to be more vigilant. Marsha goes only to the restroom and right back to her office, closing her door the second she is able. At least she didn't bring anyone else back to her office. *It would be nice if* she *would try to boost the morale a bit herself,* I think to myself.

The next several weeks go by as smoothly as can be hoped for. There are no more cuts. Four of us are still working overtime, but the routine is getting more manageable. Or maybe we are just getting more numb to it. The paychecks have been very nice, and I've spruced up my apartment a bit. Spring is starting to break, and I am excited to spend some more time with Zanna and Emily. We've had a few dinner outings, but with my work schedule and their families,

72

finding the time has been challenging.

I am pleased to step back and look at my life. My saving account is growing, I have talked with Charles, Courtney, and Anthony once over drinks, and I have been developing somewhat of a relationship with Adam, though solely over text messages. I am exhausted, but I'm happy. I think.

Today is Friday, and I am excited to join Emily and her family for pizza night at her place. Her home smells of warm garlic, and I am greeted with hugs from all sides when I walk through the doorway. Knocking is not needed when you are as close as family. The sense of togetherness is intoxicating. An ache of my own loneliness rears its head for just a minute before I am able to muffle it. I am happy for my friend and grateful to be included.

The home cooked pizza and dessert of gooey fudge brownies are delicious, and I eat more than my stomach should hold. We laugh, talk with the kids about their day, and just enjoy being together. I am able to join Emily in the children's bedtime routine. Reading a silly story, saying our prayers, and kissing them goodnight fills me up in a way that I have been missing for so long.

Once the house is quiet, Emily and I cozy up on her couch with fuzzy, warm blankets. We catch up on our busy lives. When I fill her in on the changes at my job, a look of concern shows on her face. After a pause, she starts, "Is this what you want? Are these long hours and deception making you happy?". I am a little taken aback. "Deception?" I was avoiding thinking of it like this. "Well, you have information that your co-workers might want or need to know. This side of you that is hiding information for personal gain is new and different."

"This is business, Emily," I rationalize. "I have to make hard choices in order to advance. I need to look out for myself, you know." "Yes, but at what cost? Don't lose who you are." Slightly bothered, I tell her I will be careful and then change the subject. The rest of the night is fun and rejuvenating, but I can't shake the annoyance that I am being judged for doing my job.

This weekend, I try to busy myself with cleaning the apartment, getting groceries, and other mundane adult tasks. By Sunday, I'm in need of a change of scenery, so I head to the office for just a few hours. It wouldn't hurt to get a head start on the week.

When I arrive, the first thing I notice is that the light in Marsha's office is on. I don't want to startle her, so I clear my throat and make a little extra noise getting settled into my desk and getting situated. My computer starts to hum awake, and I look around the dim office and replay what Emily said last night. I remind myself that there are many worse things I could be doing, and earning some extra money is much better than wallowing alone at home.

"Lydia, what are you doing here?" I turn to see Marsha walking towards me. She looks so different in her casual outfit, leggings and a long top with her hair thrown up in a bun on top of her head. She isn't wearing any make up, which makes her look even more tired than usual. "I just thought I'd get a head start on the week. It will help me to keep up with our clients better. Plus, they might like to see responses to their emails dated on a weekend; they'll see that we provide thorough support." I'm really laying it on thick here.

Marsha smiles and asks if I want a coffee, this time from the break room. I follow her and wonder what request she might make of me next. I pick a cinnamon flavor coffee pod with vanilla creamer. Marsha has dark roast, black. Figures.

We make the usual pleasantries. Marsha comments that it's nice to have someone else around on the weekend. "Do you always work on Sundays?," I ask. "Many of them, but not all. Sometimes it's nice to get things checked off of my list while there's no one else here," she answers, and then quickly adds, "While the whole group isn't here I mean." This is even more awkward than I expected.

"Actually, Lydia, it is really perfect timing for you to be here. I have a project for you that the others don't need to have a heads up on. Seeing us talk may just start up the rumor mill, and that doesn't benefit anyone." *Here it comes*, I think. I shouldn't have come in. This secrecy is giving me indigestion. I'm not so sure I'm cut out for the business world after all.

"We have been holding up alright since we've been able to cut costs so much. And while it's unfortunate that some had to be let go, our clients are still getting service and the business is saving an incredible amount of money."

I think of what Emily said and take a deep breath. "Some....you mean Beverly, Addison, Michael and Bruce? I'm happy to know that we're doing well, but I'm afraid this isn't sustainable, Marsha." "It's best not to think of it like that, Lydia," she answers curtly. I wonder if I've already said too much. Will I be the next to go? Will one person take on the job I was doing for two people in addition to their own? When will this stop?

"You have to think of what is best for the business. If we let four, or better yet five workers go, we will be able to keep all of the rest of the team employed." She isn't wrong. This is better than the business closing and everyone being let go. But wait. "Five?," I quietly ask.

"Yes, five. One more will put us where we need to be. And I think you are just the person to do it."

"Do what?" I'm afraid to hear the response.

"You need to take next week to see who is not doing well and who is able to pick up the slack. Use some tact so the person you chose to let go doesn't know what is happening right away. That way they will more easily work with his or her replacement. That will be the most efficient and least stressful transition for everyone." Marsha's eyes are piercing, and I have to turn away.

"No, I can't do that! Besides, how could I make a good decision? I don't know how the others are doing!" I realize I may be acting too gruff. I need to say the right things so I don't end up like Beverly, Addison, Michael, and Bruce. I take a deep breath. "Thank you for thinking of me. I appreciate that you see the hard work I've been putting in. I know you've been so busy, too" I hope my last minute groveling isn't futile.

"There is something in this for you, Lydia." I am nervous but intrigued by Marsha's answer. "I'd like to move you up to a junior management role on a probationary basis. You would be given access to how your coworkers are doing, you would have the chance to be in charge of some of the employees here, and of course, you would get a nice bonus with a raise."

This is it! I knew my hard work would be recognized. I mentally start to calculate my pay raise. Maybe I could buy a house soon and get out of my horrible apartment! Remembering what I would have to do to earn this position brings me back to Earth. Emily's concern echos in my head. "Thank you Marsha. I am so excited for this opportunity. Can we talk more this week?"

"Of course. This is a big decision. You should think about this, *about your future*, carefully before you decide. But I will need an answer by next Monday," Marsha says with thinly veiled annoyance at my inability to commit immediately. She lifts up her styrofoam coffee mug as if to cheers, and walks back to her office without another word.

Back at my desk, I wonder if this offer is only because Marsha is tired of being the bad guy. She has had to let four people go in just a few weeks. I am elated at the chance to earn more money. Money buys freedom and opportunity, and Lord knows I could use both right now. But I can't shake the feeling that I'm selling my soul by crossing over to management in this way. I feel like a traitor to my coworkers and to myself.

I muddle through a few emails, and then sit back and sigh deeply. I don't know what to do. I should make a pros and cons list. I should call Zanna and Emily. I wish I could talk to my mom. But I don't do any of these things. Instead, I get out my phone and text Adam. I ask how he is, and he responds so quickly, I wonder if he was re-reading our previous conversations. He tells me how he went hiking again today with friends. What an adventurous life he leads! After a few messages about the beautiful scenery he saw and the hearty appetite he worked up, he asks me about my day. I give him the overview of my day so far. There is a short pause, and he types, *Come see me this weekend. It will help to work this out in person.*

As has happened many times since investigating the picture of my dad, I nearly drop my phone in surprise. This is not something the old Lydia would agree to. This man could be anyone. He could be unsafe. But I'm not the same Lydia I was before. I'm ready for a change, for a chance to think this work thing through, and for answers about my dad. Maybe I will be able to find some adventure of my own along the way.

I breathe deeply once again and respond, *Yes. Where should we meet?*

The response is simple but powerful.

Four Hundred Sycamore.

14 Disoriented and confused

Ok.

These two letters over text are all it takes to get me closer to the answers that I have been waiting for. I tell myself that I knew all along that my patience would win out and that Adam would finally share what he knows. But I really didn't know. There was a part of me that gave up after the first time he changed the subject. I am relieved. I am afraid.

I spend just one more hour at work. It's all I can do with how much my mind is spiraling in all directions right now. I know my lack of focus will be showing in my work. Instead of forcing myself to keep going, I decide to trudge home and hope that the walk and fresh air will help to calm the tingling nerves that feel like pin pricks up and down my arms.

Adam and I talk a bit more. It's clear that he is afraid that a line has been crossed. He went from telling me all of the details of his weekend to short and spaced out messages. It doesn't matter though. We make a plan, and on Saturday morning, we will each be making the drive to Four Hundred Sycamore Road, Layton, Utah. I will see the place in the picture for myself and meet Adam in person. I should be afraid of getting hurt or kidnapped, but I feel strangely close to Adam. As I think this to myself, I remember that I made this name up. I really don't know anything about him. He could be catfishing me and putting me in danger. I can't bring myself to worry about this though. My mind is completely focused on the picture, on my dad, and on what I may learn about Gregory Burke. I know this is the right decision. It just has to be.

I wonder if I should tell Emily and Zanna, but when I grab my phone to text them, I see that it is after 11:00. They will both be asleep by now, and I should think this through before saying anything anyhow. I go through the motions of getting ready for bed, but I know my attempts are futile. Sleep will not be coming easy tonight.

The week crawls along like a turtle running underwater. My stomach is in knots, and I don't know where to turn. Every part of my life is anxiety-ridden. I do my best to keep my head down and just keep working harder. If I exhaust myself during the day, maybe I can sleep at night and the weekend will come faster.

By Friday night, I am a wreck. My eyes are dark and heavy, and I look like I've aged ten years. I was able to avoid nearly everyone at work by getting there early, staying late, and skipping breaks. It is possible that the others are avoiding me, too, because they are afraid of what this week has done to me. I have to stop now. I need to rest so I can be on top of my game tomorrow. For the first time in over a year, I stop at the store to get a sleep aid. There's no need to shop for dinner; I'm not able to eat anyhow. I shed my clothes at the door, grab a bottle of water, and down the sleeping pill. Just the possibility of turning my mind off in a medicated haze allows me to relax even before the medicine hits. Soon, I am asleep. But the dreams are all but blocked out. They are enhanced. Vivid. Powerful.

There is screaming. Yelling? Maybe it's an argument, because I hear at least two voices. My body is filled with terror and confusion, and I'm not able to see anything. It is so dark and hot. Blankets cover my body. There are so many blankets that I struggle to get out. I am suffocating. Sweat pools around me, and I claw to find any opening for fresh air. The yelling grows louder, and I am certain that it's my mother's voice. She is angry, afraid, and sad. I can't distinguish the other voices, but I know that there are at least two more. They aren't familiar. I need to breathe. The yelling escalates until I hear the *thud* of the slamming door.

The noise is actually just me, landing on the floor with a *thud*, and I find myself panting in a mess of blankets and pillows. It is dark, and like the dream that surrounded me moments ago, so does the sweat, terror, and confusion. I peer around my blacked out room and see that the only bits of light are coming from the red *12:35am* of my clock. This is going to be a long night. I am drenched, and the yelling in my dream continues to circle around my brain. I remind myself that this must be the effects of the sleep aid, but it doesn't help to calm the fear that I still feel. Where did these thoughts come from? I feel dizzy and struggle to get back into bed. It doesn't take long until I am asleep again.

I am in a speeding car, and the neighborhood outside is a blurred mass of blues, greens, and beiges. Rain is pouring and the *thwap thwap* of the wipers is keeping time with the ragged sobs coming from the driver in the front seat. "Where are we going?," I yell while trying to brace myself from sliding across the bench seat of the old station wagon I find myself in. The seats are a blue vinyl and the smell is of pine air freshener. "Slow down!" I'm not sure that I say

81

these words out loud, because I am too busy being thrown to the other side of the seats as we round the next curve at a sickening speed. *This is a dream*, I tell myself. We are heading right towards a house with trees directly in our path. *This isn't real.* I throw my arms up to protect my face and brace myself. *You have to wake up.* The tires screech as they try to brake on the wet macadam. *Wake up, wake up!* The car slides sideways to barely miss the trees, so close that and I can see their new buds forming. The white shutters of the cottage house in front of me blur as rain washes down the windows. I slide forward towards the back of the driver's seat in front of me but am finally held back by the thick seatbelt that didn't exist a few seconds ago. The car stops, but I can't escape the seatbelt. I'm stuck, and the seat belt is growing wider across my body with every second. Soon, it is covering me, holding me against the sticky seat, squeezing the air from my lungs.

I wake up in the same spot I was earlier, choking on my blankets that have wound so tightly around my body. I can't imagine what I must have looked like, thrashing around in my sleep. The clock shows 3:29am. I was asleep for longer than I expected. The sleep aid worked by knocking me unconscious, but I'm not sure the trade off was worth it. I feel groggy and my head hurts. My eyes burn with exhaustion, but I'm too afraid to go back to sleep.

Instead, I turn on the shower as hot as I can stand it. Once it heats up and steam fills the room, I step under the scalding water and try to shake the images and sounds out of my head. I stand under the flowing water for a very long time. Eventually, the water cools and so does my terror. When I see that it is almost 5:00, I say a silent prayer that my water bill won't be outrageous, and then hope that the nightmare-inducing medicine I took is out of my system. I know that I need to drive in just a few hours, and I need to be able to function. I check that my alarm is still set, calm myself, and hope to sleep for just a little longer.

When the alarm sounds, I am disoriented and confused. I realize I was able to sleep a blessedly dreamless sleep. I am thankful that I'm already showered, but sleeping on wet hair has done little to allow me to get ready quickly. Tufts of blonde stick out in all directions. It will take an act of God to get it to behave. I put as much effort as I can muster into taming the mess on top of my head before making the rest of myself presentable.

In just a short time, I will meet Adam for the first time, and I will see the house in the picture of my dad with my own eyes. To say I'm nervous is an enormous understatement. The fact that I am overworked, sleep deprived, shaken from nightmares, and on top of that, lonely, does not help. I should eat something, but I know I'm not able. I pour coffee into a to-go mug, grab a granola bar just in case, and do a once-over to make sure I am ready.

Of course I'm not ready for this, but I'm as close as I will get. Once I'm in my car, I type into the GPS with shaking hands: 400 Sycamore Road, Layton. The robotic voice starts to give commands as if this is just like any other drive. I tell myself that it *is* like any other drive, and that I can turn around at any time if I want. I know I won't, but it is comforting to know that I do have the option. This, at least, is something I can control.

I fiddle with the radio and play the drums on my steering wheel. I change the station every few minutes with a severe lack of focus. As I get closer, I realize I haven't told anyone where I'm going. I may be meeting a serial killer for all I know. My heart nearly beats out of my chest, and I reach for my phone. I tap out a quick message to Zanna and Emily: *Meeting Adam at 400 Sycamore.*

Seconds later, my phone rings, and I see Emily's picture filling the screen. "Hello?," I say quietly. "You should have told me! I would have come with you! You shouldn't do this alone!," Emily's shrill voice shouts into my ear. I turn the volume down on my phone and try to calm her down. Focusing on her worry helps me to forget my own for a few minutes. I tell her about the last few days at work, my nightmares, and my plans for the morning. She is audibly not pleased to hear about any of these things. "I'm worried about you, Lydia. I mean, I'm happy that you are stepping out of your comfort zone a little, but maybe you aren't doing it in the safest way." "Adam is safe. I can't describe why I know this, but I just do," I try to rationalize with her.

We talk for a few more minutes, and she only lets me hang up after I promise to share my location until I'm on my way home. It's a compromise from her initial request to call or text every 10 minutes. I reassure her, and we say our goodbyes. Once I get to a stop light only three minutes from my destination, I turn on location services on my phone to share with Zanna and Emily. Zanna was a little late to the game in her response, but she is happy to know where I am, too.

As I enter the neighborhood, my nerves return in full force. I tremble slightly as my eyes scan the numbers on the mailboxes. The neighborhood is quaint, though a bit dated, with split level houses and overgrown maple trees. The sun is shining and the early spring grass is showing through bits of leftover snow. The numbers creep higher and finally, I reach 400. The house with the blue mailbox and white shutters from my dad's picture and last night's dream looms in front of me. I stand next to my car and stare from across the street. My feelings are complex, and I'm not sure where to start with them. I don't have time though, because I hear a car door close behind me.

A handsome blonde steps away from his obviously worn and well-loved Jeep, a mountain bike tethered to the tailgate. He is dressed simply, in jeans and a green henley shirt. "Lydia?" Words evade me, but I am able to nod my head, though nearly imperceptibly. He takes a few steps towards me, his long stride covering the short distance quickly. He takes his sunglasses off, and his blue eyes look as nervous as I feel.

He holds out his hand. "Hi, I'm Alex."

15 Cinnamon and sweet cream

I stare at him, unblinking. *Alex? This is Alex? The boy from the picture?* All of the thoughts swirl round and round in my head, but none of them are able to escape through my lips. Alex shifts nervously, then pulls his hand back to wipe his sweaty palm on his jeans. "I'm sorry. I should have told you before," he mumbles, keeping his head down and averting his eyes. "I...I... What?," I stammer. *Of course you should have told me before. It should have been the first thing you said!*

I may not be able to speak, but I am able to move. I turn back to my car and grab the door handle. "Lydia, wait!" I'm not sure why I pause. "At least look around a bit. Isn't this what you've been searching for?" He isn't wrong. Will I just have more questions if I leave here right now? I know that I will, and I can't risk any more sleepless nights.

I find my voice. "You lied to me." Adam...I mean, Alex...starts to answer, and then stops. He regroups and tries again. "Well, not technically. I didn't say anything about who I am." *Is this guy serious?* "Lying by omission is still lying," I snap. He nods his head ever so slightly. His voice is low and his eyes are downcast when he answers.

"You're right. But you have to understand. I needed to know why you had a picture of me. It's not everyday you find someone searching for answers about a picture of you."

He has a point. I would have probably done the same thing, if I had even responded at all. Maybe I would have called the police. It adds up, but I am shaken. He isn't who I thought he was. "Right," I say slowly. "Well Alex, I'm Lydia." I reach out to finally return his handshake. It is awkward and neither of us know when to let go, so we end up almost holding hands for a few seconds.

"So," I say when I finally have my hand back, but I stop when I'm not sure what to say next. Luckily, Alex is more resilient that I am. "Your dad helped us move into this house, many years ago. When did you say he, um, died?" *What was that pause in his voice?* He knows more than he is sharing.

"He died when I was five, so 25 years ago," I share cautiously. "That must have been right after we moved into this house. We lived here up until about 10 years ago. We probably shouldn't snoop too close, since it looks like the new owners are home."

There is a white truck in the driveway and a light is visible through the shear curtains that must open to the living room. "It's weird to see this place again," Alex reminisces. "I haven't been back here since I moved. I'm happy to see that the new owners seem to be taking care of it". The sidewalks are free of snow and ice, and the porch is clean, with charming decorations that show us that the owners are eager for spring to start. The sun is shining, which makes this house look like a true home. "Were you happy here?," I ask Alex. "Yes!," he eagerly responds.

He points to a maple tree in the front yard. "I had a piñata hanging from that branch on my 9th birthday, and over there," he motions to

87

the end of the driveway, "that's where I fell off my bike and cut my knee up. I bled through my favorite blue sweatpants and needed stitches. I'll never forget how upset my mom was." He laughs to himself, and his unfocused eyes tell me he is not completely present right now.

I look at the tree and remember it from my dream. The dream was so vivid and surprisingly accurate. "Do you remember meeting me?," I ask, wondering if the dream could have really been a resurfacing memory. Alex startles and looks at me with an expression that could be fear. "No," he says definitively. "I would have remembered that." *That's a strange answer*, I think to myself. "I dreamt about this house last night. I know I've studied that picture a thousand times, but my dream had more details than I would have gotten from one picture." Alex shrugs and changes the subject. "Should we walk around the neighborhood?," he asks. The sun is out and the air has more than a hint of spring. A walk will do me some good. Plus, now that I'm here, I'm not quite ready to leave.

"I'm not sure what I was expecting to learn today," I confess. "The people here wouldn't know him from so long ago. You barely remember him, and we have photographic proof that you've met." Alex shrugs again, and then returns to reminiscing about the place where he called home for most of his childhood. He shows me where his friends used to live, takes me to his old bus stop, and points out the trees he used to climb. "I fell out of that one over there," he points. "It was a lot smaller then, I'm sure, but it is huge in my memory. My mom thought I broke my arm for sure, but it was just bruised." He is smiling as he thinks about her.

"Where is she now?," I ask. "Oh, near me," Alex answers. "When I left for college in Colorado, they downsized to a smaller place. I moved back closer to them after I graduated." "They?," I ask. It's a silly question, but I envisioned him living with just his mother. "Yeah,

my parents are still there. It's nice being close, but not *too* close, you know?" I *don't* know. I've never lived close to my father, and I would give anything to be with my mother right now. "Yeah," I lie.
Alex notices and changes the subject. "There's a great coffee place down the road. Do you want to go there and warm up?" "I would, actually. I didn't realize that the chill was sneaking up on me. I guess it's not quite spring yet."

We head back to our cars, and he gives me the address to put in my GPS. I remember that I didn't take my phone with me, and somehow, we've been looking at the house and neighborhood for almost an hour. I'm not surprised to see four texts and one missed call from Emily. Zanna is a little less anxious with only one message. I plug in the address, send a quick thumbs up text, and shift into drive. My stomach rumbles to remind me that I haven't eaten yet today.

The café is small and cozy. It smells of cinnamon and sweet cream. As soon as the scent hits my nose, my stomach rumbles again, this time louder. Alex laughs and nudges me, "Ok, brunch with coffee then." It's such a simple motion, but it's comfortable and natural. It should feel odd to have a stranger treat me like this. I order a vanilla latte and a cinnamon bun, the heavenly scent having sapped me of any willpower. Alex nods in approval and asks for the same.

The café is moderately filled. Couples are sipping their teas and mochas while little kids enjoy hot chocolate and warm pastries. The music is nearly inaudible, but it's just enough to fill any silence that may creep up. A crackling fireplace burns invitingly in the back, and we find a table nearby. Conversation comes easily as we talk about the day. I fill Alex in on work, and he asks how I'm feeling about all of it. I confess that I'm uneasy, but that accepting the promotion seems like the right move. "That makes sense." Then he adds, "But don't settle. I can tell you're a hard worker, and any company would be lucky to have you." "Thanks," I smile. This makes me feel better. It's not the black and white decision I was hoping we would come to, but it is helpful.

The plates that used to hold cinnamon buns appear to be licked clean. They were perfect in every way, and part of me wishes I asked for two. Once the dense, warm dough starts to settle in my stomach, I am hit with a wave of exhaustion. I should head home before I'm too tired to drive. Alex agrees that he needs to get going soon, too. He tells me he is meeting a few friends to mountain bike soon, and he hopes the pastry doesn't slow him down. "You live an adventurous life. It's great that you have friends to do things like mountain bike with. I can't imagine Zanna on a mountain bike!". I laugh out loud just thinking about it. "You should come with us sometime!," Alex says excitedly. "Me?! No. I can mountain bike about as well as Zanna." I laugh again, though this is probably funnier to me than to Alex. "Well, then for a hike. A group of us are going to check out some new trails next weekend. You'd like them....the people *and* the trails." I hesitate. Before I can decline, he says, "We'll pick an easy one. Next Saturday at 9am. I'll send you the address." He's out of his chair before I can respond.

16 What a hypocrite

The drive home is easier than the ride up, but with all of the morning's adrenaline out of my system, I am struggling to stay awake. Now is the perfect time to call Emily and Zanna to fill them in and let them know I'm safe. They both answer the conference call, Emily audibly more relieved and Zanna more excited. I tell them about the house, the neighborhood, and then the most important part: Adam is actually Alex.

"You are kidding me. And he didn't even tell you until you were there in person! You should have gotten in your car, Lydia. You can't trust him!" Emily is not pleased to say the least. "I know, I know. I had the same reaction. My hand was on the handle to get back in the car, but I couldn't leave without knowing more," I say. "So why was he with your dad? How did he know him?," Zanna jumps in. "He says he must have helped him move, way back then. That's it. There's nothing else."

My last statement is as much of a realization to me as it is information to them. "I guess this is it. There's no story. I was just grasping at anything to be close to a family that I no longer have."

Emily is quick to comfort. "I'm so sorry Lydia. You will always have us." My friends are lifesavers, and I know I am so lucky to have them. To make the conversation more upbeat, I tell them about the hiking plans we have for next week. "I think I'd like to go. It would be something different." Zanna is excited. "Yes! Take lots of pictures!" Emily is surprised. "Really? I figured you'd be done with Alex now that you have closure."

We talk it out, but there really isn't any explaining it. I felt safe today, even happy. I felt like my old self. I'm nervous and unsure of what it will be like, meeting new people in such an adventurous setting, but I am sure that I will be going. I just hope I can keep up!

On Monday morning, I head straight into Marsha's office and tell her that I'm ready to accept the promotion. I see elation flash across her face, but she covers it up quickly with a professional hand shake. She looks very different today compared to how she did last weekend. Her hair is up in a severe bun and her pantsuit is ironed to a T. "I'm so glad to hear this, Lydia," she says, a little too eagerly. "Why don't you get settled in here, and I'll work to get you access to the information portals. We can start your first project today."

"Thank you!" I'm excited to jump right in. I pull a chair to a small space on the edge of her desk. "What is the project? I have some ideas that might increase productivity." Marsha looks at me a little confused. "Your first project is to review the numbers and see who can be cut. We talked about this." I am embarrassed, but also instantly let down. I want this opportunity to be more. "Right. I didn't realize it would be so quick. I'll grab my things and be right back."

I walk to my desk and pray to be invisible, but it doesn't work. Courtney is at my cubicle only three seconds after I get there. "What was that about?" My stomach clenches. I am the worst liar, but I know I can't tell the truth. "Marsha asked me to work on a project with her today. I'm getting set up in there so she can tell me about it." That's not really lying. Though what did I say to Alex just this weekend? *Lying by omission is still lying. What a hypocrite*, I think to myself. Courtney buys the line and wishes me luck. I know she is hoping I'm not getting fired. I'm hoping I don't have to fire her.

I sit with Marsha as she gives me access to programs with more personnel information than I need to know. Ages, salaries, years of service, all right here at my finger tips. It feels like such an invasion of privacy. Sooner than I expected, Marsha leaves my computer to go back to hers. We feels it's better for me to work in her office today so no one can see my screen. It's the right decision, but it makes my new role feel even more sneaky.

Quickly, I'm able to do the math. I see where the weakest link is and who should be able to pick up the slack. Jennifer has been with the company for six years. She has been here longer than several of the others, so her salary cut will be beneficial to the company. Her numbers have slowly been slipping too. I don't know her well, but I know her young children have been trading off the flu, stomach bugs, and any other ailment common in elementary school. She has to juggle caring for them as well as working, and I know this is why she hasn't been as productive here. Knowing this background makes me double check the calculations, but it's black and white; Jennifer has to be the next to go.

Cal, on the other hand, is newer to the company and therefore has a lower salary. His numbers aren't the highest, but they are steadily climbing. This makes me think he can handle Jennifer's tasks in addition to his own. Maybe by rewarding him early in his career, he will be motivated to work even harder.

I sit back and sigh. I do not like this first project. Marsha looks up, and I see the worry lines settling across her forehead and under her eyes. She has been looking more and more stressed over the past few months. Her wardrobe has taken a step in the other direction, becoming more and more professional. I know she has been working on the weekends. I wonder how hard she is working to prove herself worthy of her job.

"Well?," Marsha asks me, rather harshly. She softens when she sees my surprise. "How is it going?" "I think I've found the best choices." I tell her about the two employees and support my reasoning. Without double checking my work, she says, "Yes, that's the right call. Talk with Cal today please." "Today? Can I have a little time to catch up, to go over what I'll say?" I know we're under a lot of strain, but I expect a little more time. *Jennifer would probably like a little more time, too.* The knot in my stomach tightens even more, and I wonder if I'm developing an ulcer.

Marsha is taken aback by my hesitation. "I can take over your first task after your promotion if you really want me to...," she trails off. "No. No, I can do this." "Good," she answers before I can take another breath. "Let me clear a few things up and you can use my office. There's no sense stewing over it. I can see that it's already weighing on you."

I don't want Marsha to think I can't handle this, so I take a deep breath and mentally, quickly, go over what I will say to Cal. I remember the conversation Marsha had with me when she asked me to shadow Beverly. I try to remember what parts went well and what parts sat poorly with me. In less than five minutes, Marsha is out of the office and I am alone. I sit in the silence for a minute or two and listen to the ringing in my ears that suggests I am overwhelmed.

There are many things about what Marsha is doing that I don't agree with, but she wasn't wrong in thinking I should get this over with. I am grateful for the promotion, but I can't help but feel this is just for me to do Marsha's dirty work. Maybe this is how anyone has to move up in the business world.

I walk over to Cal and ask him to join me in Marsha's office. Courtney looks up at me quizzically. There's no going back now. She knows I've crossed over.

The conversation with Cal goes well. I am pleased and relieved, but only temporarily. In two more days, I'll have to meet with Jennifer. By then she will know what is coming, and I'm sure it won't go as smoothly. Marsha returns to the office with only an insincere question about how it went. She doesn't even say anything to Cal before she comes in. She jumps into the next project, which is much more comfortable for me. She provides me with a relatively open-ended task on budgets, numbers, and supplies. It is hard work and there is a lot of it, but at least I don't have to face the others. This must be why Marsha has been holed up in her office 95% of the time.

The next time I look up, I see that the lights are dim and it is only Marsha and me. I pack up, emotionally and physically exhausted, and head home. Only four more days until the weekend.

I chat back and forth on one text strand with Zanna and Emily and another with Alex. They are my saving graces each night while I once again fall into the habit of take-out food and slumping on the couch.

On Wednesday morning, I move into a spare utility closet-turned-office for more privacy. There is one tiny window and room for no more than one desk, two chairs, and possibly a small shelf. The sterile eggshell walls and solid wooden door make it feel like a jail cell rather than a private office. As I look around, I don't allow myself to think that this seems like a step down. Rather, I try to focus on what I can do to make it more livable. I envision a few pictures of Zanna, Emily, and me on a small shelf, maybe next to a small vase with a fake flower. There's barely any natural light in here; no living plant would survive for more than a few days. I shudder to think that I may not survive for more than a few days either.

After a rushed morning of relocating, emails, phone calls, and headaches, there's a knock at my nearly closed door. Jennifer peaks her head in. "Marsha said you wanted to talk to me?," she asks nervously. I see her quickly look around, and there's just a hint of sympathy in her eyes for me in this tiny box. Noticing this only briefly distracts me from my heavy annoyance that Marsha would have sent her here to get fired without asking, or at least telling, me first.

"Oh. Yes," I say unconvincingly. "Have a seat." I motion to the only other seat in the room, a mere six inches from the doorway in which she is standing. "Jennifer, I noticed that your productivity has been slipping recently." She jumps in before I can go on. "I'm going to stay late every night starting tonight to get more done. I'll do it off the clock." "That's really generous of you, but you shouldn't have to work for free. But either way, management has been forced to make some cuts." I try to sound professional and hide the trembling that is radiating through my body. Jennifer's demeanor changes from fearful and nervous to annoyed and angry. "Management? Who, you? You've been in your new job for less than three days and you're already calling yourself management?" "No, I," I can't finish before she starts again. "Everyone knows that you sold the others out just to get a raise. But you can change that. Let me stay. Don't fire me. Please....my kids need me to keep working."

This is worse than I could have imagined. I'm letting the situation spiral out of control. Jennifer is right to question me. Who am I to make this decision and act like I'm in charge, let alone fire someone? "I'm sorry, but it's out of my hands," I say, comforting myself rather than her. Jennifer starts to cry. I look for a tissue and she snaps, "Don't bother. You've done enough already. I'll clear out my desk." She leaves, closing my door behind her, more than a touch harder than is necessary.

I feel terrible. Looking around my miniature office, I think about what has happened over the past few months. I think about how hard I've been working, the people who have been let go, and the change in culture in the office. I think of how Marsha made me think that I've earned this, while she sits in her spacious office, sunlight cascading through her enormous windows, avoiding the dirty work. I slump in the chair, determined not to go and ask for Jennifer's forgiveness. It would only seem insulting.

Somehow, I make it through the week. I firm up plans with Alex and learn that we have a four mile hike laid out for us with several of his friends. It has been so long since I've done anything remotely like this, and I'm nervous I won't know what to do. I barely have the right clothing, but I hope that my gym shoes, thick socks, and a Utes ball cap will complete the get up and help me to fit in. If I'm lucky, I may even stay warm and avoid blisters. If a miracle happens, I may even be able to keep up with the group.

Alex tells me where to meet the group and reminds me to bring water and a snack, just in case. This makes me worry that it will be an overly strenuous four miles, but he reassures me that it's just better to be prepared. I set my alarm clock, say a silent prayer to avoid insomnia, and amazingly find myself slipping off to sleep without too much time passing.

17 Not the least bit jealous

The morning is bright and cheerful, with the perfect amount of chill in the air. I'm far less nervous this morning than on the last time I made this drive, so I'm able to eat a full breakfast, complete with waffles from the freezer, strawberries, and a full mug of to-go coffee. I tell myself that I'll need the sustenance to keep up with the others today.

The drive is pleasant and not too far. I love having Zanna and Emily in my life, but it is a nice feeling to not have to depend solely on them for my social life. They have their own families and life apart from me, though they never make me feel left out. The time in the car allows me to unpack this past week or two, and the uneasiness of it all weighs on me. I am grateful for the weekend.

The trailhead is easy enough to to find, and there are a few hikers here clad in high socks and ball caps already. My nerves return as I enter into this group of unfamiliar but inviting people. I park, gather my things, and take a deep breath to calm myself. Making new friends is not my strong suit, and I pray that I'm not too awkward. *Are my clothes ok? Do I look like I'm trying too hard? What will we talk about?* Before any true panic can set in, one of the hikers strolls eagerly up to me. "Hi! Are you Lydia?," she asks with a friendly smile. "Yes, I'm friends with Alex." *Friend* seems like an odd way to describe him, but I think it's better than *guy I found on the internet.* "I'm so glad you're coming today! It's a perfect day to be outside. I'm really excited! I'm Addison." Her pep is only a little alarming, but she seems to mean well. Addison introduces the others as Alex pulls up in his Jeep, his wide smile shining bright through his windows. He hops out gracefully and makes sure that everyone knows each others' names. I hope I can remember them all.

Our group is complete at eight, and I try to be inconspicuous as my eyes take inventory of the gear everyone is bringing. Most have a small backpack water system and that's it. I think about all of the snacks, sunblock, change of clothes, and other apparently non-essentials that I had planned to bring with me. I try not to show how overpacked I am and just grab my water bottle and car key.

The hike is a little strenuous for me, but the others glide over the trails with the ease of mountain goats. They are clearly slowing their pace so I can keep up, but no one seems bothered by it at all. Conversation flows naturally from excited recounts of family, work, and weekend plans to quiet appreciation of the world around us. The crunch of our boots, wind rolling through the trees, animals shuffling by, and majestic eagles and hawks calling out as they soar above us are enough to fill our ears. I watch one hawk with an especially wide wingspan float over the expanse below us. *What must it feel like to be that free?*

I realize that these people seem free and at peace. With a deep breath and a profound appreciation for Alex's invitation today, I hike forward.

On my drive home, I am grateful for the flip-flops and snacks that I packed. My feet are speckled with budding blisters, and I worry a little for the soreness that I know I'll be feeling soon. I realize that I am smiling. It is a real, effortless smile, the kind that has been hard to come by for months now. This day was what I needed. The separation from the other parts of my life helps me to feel like myself and, for once, to feel more relaxed. I put Emily and Zanna over the car speakers and recount the day. I am so lucky to have these two who are only happy for me and not the least bit jealous that I may be making more friends.

Before I make it home, Alex texts me about next weekend's hike with his group. I am committed before I even know the details. He must know that I'm still on an endorphin high and that I would agree to almost anything right now. He tells me that it will be a bit more grueling than today, but I still want to come. We chat a little about the changing weather and how nice it feels to be outside.

As soon as I enter through the door of my apartment, the calm begins to wear off. The enclosed walls coupled with the prospect of a new work week weigh on me already. I vow to push it out of my mind for the rest of the day. Instead, I will fill the evening hours with cleaning, grocery shopping, and television. When night falls, I am able to drift off to a sound sleep more easily than any night in months.

The next morning, I wake up groggy. I roll over and jump up when I see that I slept for ten straight hours. *I can't believe this!* This sudden movement makes me feel soreness all up my back and sides. I know what's going to happen when I get out of bed, but I push myself to do it anyhow. Standing makes every muscle in my legs pull, and walking takes an enormous amount of effort. It is a feeling I haven't

experienced for a long time, and I am surprised to realize how out of shape I am. I'm instantly nervous for next weekend. I make a mental note to work even just a half hour less each day so I can have time to work up some endurance for the weekend with my new friends.
I go through the motions of the morning and start the coffee. There is nothing like the comforting smell of Columbian roast to start my day. I take a few minutes to wake up while cradling the warm mug in my hands, and I replay the previous day. I notice that I am still smiling. I grab my phone and wonder if I have any messages from Zanna, Emily, or Alex.

There are three! One is in my group chat with Zanna and Emily. Zanna sent a hilarious picture of herself in bed. Her hair is everywhere and make up is smudged around her eyes. Her daughter is sleeping across her body with her hand basically up Zanna's nose. Zanna captioned the photo "Mommy Life". It is far from flattering, but it is a true picture of love. I'm happy for her.

The next is from an unknown number. I open it and see that Alex shared my number with Addison. She says she had fun yesterday and is excited for next weekend. She attached a picture of the group, and I love how happy and carefree we all look. I even look like I fit in!

The last message makes my heart stop for a full minute when I see it. It is from "Zz Jared". I added the "Zz" part to his contact name when I moved out. I didn't want his name to show up on my contacts list unless I scrolled all the way to the end, purposely looking for him. I realize now that I haven't done this for months. *Why would he be texting me?* My mind goes through the worst case scenarios. *Is someone in his family sick? Has there been an accident?* There is no reason to torture myself with possibilities, so I dive in and open the message.

Hey Lydia, how are you?

Is he serious? That's it? After all this time, he reaches out for no clear reason and puts it on me to find out what he wants. I am disgusted and put the phone down. My mind swirls, but only a second goes by before I pick the phone back up again. I tap out a response, delete it, and then type another. *I'm good. How are you?* seems weak. *What do you want?* seems too aggressive.

Instead, I decide to text Emily and Zanna. They will know what to do. *Let's meet at Jake's Café*, was Zanna's immediate response. Emily is quick to answer too: *I can be there in 45 minutes.* I breathe a sigh of relief and turn my focus to getting myself ready rather than wondering what Jared could possibly want.

To be honest, I only try to turn my focus. It doesn't completely work, and my mind wonders from brushing my teeth to my old home with Jared. I shake my head and try to pick out clothes as I think about my old neighbors. I think about what shoes to wear and then remember the view from my back porch. The thing that strikes me about these insistent memories is that none of them directly involve Jared. The good, memorable things in my past have little to do with him.

The realization isn't enough to stop my curiosity. I grab my phone and text back. I can't help it! I need to know. *Hi Jared* is all I say. There's no sense in giving him any more information than he needs. The three bubbles showing that he is typing pop up immediately, as if he was staring at the message he sent me, waiting for me to act.

How are you?, he responds.
I'm fine. Heading out to meet friends. What's up? I want him to know I'm not sitting around pining for him.
Nothing. I was just thinking about you.

His message truly makes my stomach turn. I put my phone down and have no desire to respond.

Jake's is very busy when I arrive, and since I'm the first one of my group here, I immediately set out to find a table. There isn't any available, but I find a couple who seems to be finishing up. I stalk their table in a way that I hope isn't obvious. Emily gets there soon, and she runs over to hug me. She doesn't even wait until we've let go to ask. "Did you answer him? What do you think he wants?" We let go, and Zanna runs over before I can answer. "I can't believe that jerk has the nerve to text you out of the blue," she scowls. "I know!," I agree. "But it's just like him. He's only thinking of himself. He doesn't care what this might stir up for me."

I see the couple moving, and I ask Zanna to grab me a latte while I get the table. Soon enough, the three of us are cozied up with steaming mugs of deliciousness warming us from the inside out. The cheery coffee drinkers around us and the sunshine coming through the windows remind us that spring is upon is. Everyone is a bit perkier when the sun is out and parkas are no longer required.

I show my friends the text exchange, and Zanna pretends to gag. Emily is the first to give her opinion and thinks I should ignore the text and block his number. Zanna, of course, has a different opinion. "Let him know how amazing you are. Tell him about your promotion at work and the hiking group you joined. Make sure he knows that we're still here with you, having the time of our lives. Make him feel sorry for what he gave up."

I laugh at Zanna. Both of my friends have always had my back, albeit in different ways. I know they always will. I rationalize that I spent years committed to this man, and maybe he deserves to be heard out, though I vow that it will not change anything. I admit that I do feel a little angry, though. I have done a great job of moving past this. Then he sends one text, and here I am, calling the anguish back up. Emily puts her hand on mind and looks at me over her oversized mug. "You owe him nothing. If you want to see what he has to say, do it for you. Not for him."

The three of us put our heads together and decide to continue the conversation while we are together and have strength in numbers.

Is everything ok? is how we start. We want him to know that him thinking of me has no bearing on my life now.
Once again, he immediately begins to type. *I'm ok. I was just wondering how you are.*
Liar. *I'm doing well. Work is good. I went on a hike with a group of friends yesterday. Zanna and Emily are doing well too.* There three of us decide that this is more then enough information. We purposely don't add a question to allow the conversation to take a natural end. Jared doesn't let this happen. Instead, he takes us all by surprise. *Good, I'm glad. Can we get a drink sometime?*

It is just like him to ignore the things that I said and focus on his needs. But I have to admit, I'm curious. I decide to answer, *Let me think about it.* A simple *ok* is his only response.

Emily, Zanna, and I put our phones away and continue on with our time together. We catch up on life, family, work, and everything in between. Soon, our mugs are drained and our table is in demand. We decide to continue our day together and take a walk while the weather is good. The weather in Utah is perfect in the spring. The sun is warm, but not too hot, too soon. The air has a touch of winter remaining, allowing it to feel clear with the scent of fresh, new beginnings. The sidewalk is bustling with people who are eager to experience this as well. Families are out in droves, and for once, this doesn't make me feel sad or lonely. I look at my friends and intertwine my arms in theirs, smiling as we walk together.

Before we part, we have one more small talk about the Jared texts. I decide that I want to hear him out. I know I don't owe him anything, but I want to know I'm taking the high road by not holding any more grudges. I'm not sure that this is true yet, but I need to prove to myself that I am able to put the past in the past. I pull my phone from my pocket and reply, *Sure. Friday at Pints on Pine?* This fairly upscale bar is not far from my office and is within walking distance from my apartment. It is public and usually busy. This way, I can easily get home when I want to, and the crowd on a Friday evening will stand in the way of any intimate feelings.

He replies, *I can't wait.* I roll my eyes and hug my friends goodbye. I'm happy to feel the changes I've made since being on my own. I vow not to text Jared anymore.

18 Classy, with the right amount of lighting

This week at work is terrible! My coworkers resent me, and Marsha is treating me like a workhorse. I find solace in my cubbyhole of an office, but between this place and my apartment, I'm really just alternating between small, poorly lit prison cells by myself. I have been able to carve out a little bit of time for myself though, and I promise myself to go for a walk, go to the gym, or do something physical after work each day. Some days, Zanna or Emily join me. This light at the end of the tunnel helps, and so does my paycheck. I have been able to pay off a large chuck of my credit card bill that I racked up by furnishing my place. My dingy belongings don't look like much, but the credit card companies don't care. I even start setting aside some cash to replace my laptop.

Friday comes with little relief. I trade the stress of work for the stress of my meeting with Jared. I call it a meeting in my head because what else could this be? It certainly isn't a date. It isn't even drinks between friends. He has tried to chat with me a bit through the week, but I made sure that I've been too busy. The only message of consequence was the suggestion of meeting at 6:00. I tell him that this is a good time, because I'll come right from work. I don't want him thinking I will be going home to get myself ready.

Even so, I make sure that I look my best on Friday. The bags under my eyes and the tired expression that seems to be a permanent fixture on my face will have to stay. However, I put a little more effort in looking presentable, first for work, and then with a few finishing touches after my last email is sent. I have on semi-form-fitting black dress pants, pumps with a small heel, and a new green sweater that I treated myself to with my raise. I freshen up my mascara, add a few swipes of blush, and blot on a tiny bit of lipstick. After I run a brush through my hair, the look is complete. I tell myself that this look is for me and for no one else, and I hope I am not lying.

The street lights are already on, but the sun hasn't completely set. It is refreshing to have noticeably longer days. There is still a chill in the air, so I wrap my favorite spring jacket and my navy knitted scarf a little tighter. I think it's the chill that is making me shiver rather than nervous energy. The walk is good for me and allows me to calm down. I'm grateful for the few times I've exercised lately, because otherwise, walking a few blocks in heels would have been more of a challenge. Thank goodness I suggested a place that is so close.

I reach the door and take a deep breath as I grab the handle. *I can do this. I owe him nothing and can leave at any time.* The tactfully upbeat music fills my ears with the opening of the door, but the sound dissolves immediately as I see Jared already at the bar, the seat next to him saved. I falter and say a silent prayer of thanks that he hasn't yet noticed me. With a few calming breaths and the prospect of a martini, I regain my courage and stride over.

"Hi Jared," I say as I pull the chair out for myself. Even if he would have seen me coming, I know he wouldn't have pulled it out for me. It wouldn't have even crossed his mind. He startles, and I'm admittedly a bit pleased to have caught him off guard. The bar is classy with the right amount of lighting. The top tier liquor bottles are backlit and displayed at eye level and higher. The bartender is handsome, with a smoothly shaved head and 5 o'clock shadow. He is wearing a light pink dress shirt with the top button undone. It suits him well. He notices me as soon as I move my chair out, and he slides over a cocktail napkin.

"What will it be, miss?" Thank goodness he said miss and not ma'am. The immediate service is timed well, allowing me to confidently order a martini, and then adjust it to a Gibson. Tonight is about feeling strong, and the bite of the onion will be a nice distraction from the conversation to help me focus on myself.

The bartender gives me an impressed smile and goes to work making the drink with only the slightest bit of show. I wonder for a fraction of a moment if I should tell the bartender that this is not a date, just in case. Before I can go further with that fairy tale, Jared seems to gather his composure. He tries to give me hug while I am in the process of sitting down. It ends up being an awkward half hug, half one-armed bro-tap with him suddenly standing while I am sitting. "Lydia, it's so good to see you."

I want to be polite. I am relieved to know there isn't any hostility on my end anymore. Anger would mean that I'm holding on, and I no longer am. This realization is an empowering feeling. "It's nice to see you too, Jared. How are you?" He puts on a smile that only tugs on my heart a tiny bit. He looks attractive as always, obviously trying to look his best in a well-fitting blue polo and khaki pants. He is wearing what used to by my favorite cologne. Something is off though.

"I'm good. Work is fine and the house is ok. It's a lot more upkeep with just me though." He laughs awkwardly. *Just him? What about Monica?* I picture the two of them in the home that he and I built together, then push it from my mind. "Oh, yeah. Having an apartment has the perk of much less to maintain." It isn't really a lie, but to say anything nice about where I'm living other than the commute is a bit of a stretch.

We make pleasantries for while and I try to pace myself with my drink. Losing my composure would not be good tonight. Jared wants to order food, and I suggest only appetizers. I need to eat, but I am really not interested in a full meal with him. We place the order. I ask for a water.

He works to continue the conversation as if we are old friends. It annoys me. "Jared, what's wrong? Why did you want to meet me tonight?" Part of me is still worried something is wrong with him or his family. Maybe someone is sick. Maybe Jared lost his job or needs money or is moving. "I, well, I just wanted to see you. I needed to see you. Lydia, I made a huge mistake."

Right at that moment, the bartender brings our orders of clams casino and bruschetta. I immediately order a second Gibson. "Yes, you did," I respond confidently, "but why now? What did you think would come out of tonight? And more importantly, where's Monica?" I take a big gulp of my water, anticipating my next drink and trying to stay in control.

Jared looks around, clearly uneasily. He drops his voice, and I have to lean in to hear him. "Monica was a mistake. I know that now. I just want to go back to the way things were." I am stunned. For months, I longed to hear these words. Now, they sound so pitiful that I almost laugh. But I don't, because the only feelings I have for this man now are those that resemble sympathy. His attempt at looking nice suddenly appears faded and ragged. The bags under his eyes are more visible than my own. I remind myself that we were happy once, and while "we" will never be again, there is no reason to twist the knife. There is also no reason to drag myself through this again. "I'm sorry Jared, but we are past that. I'm sorry that you're hurting, but it's time to move on. That can be with Monica or…" "I don't want Monica," he says sharply. "Ok, it can be with someone else or no one at all." The bartender brings my drink. I take a small sip, and the onion is bitter on my tongue. "It just can't be with me."

Jared looks up at me, clearly having expected that I would come running back to him. This is my cue to leave. I look at my watch to give him a little bit of grace, suggesting that I just have somewhere else to be. I put more than my share of cash on the bar, take one more slow, long draw of my drink, and stand up. "Don't go. We have so much more to catch up on. You didn't even tell me about your new friends yet." He looks pitiful. "I have to go. Good luck, Jared." I grab my purse and head to the door, trying not to run, and with no desire to look back.

I wait until I'm at least a block away before pulling out my phone. I had my phone on silent, but Zanna and Emily didn't care. They sent about 25 messages filled with varying amounts of encouragement, rage, and comedic relief. I smile and dial them both. They answer in about 0.5 seconds and immediately start talking over each other, asking questions about the night. I feel like a weight that I didn't know I was carrying has been lifted from my shoulders. I replay the evening and have to remind myself that this really happened. This wasn't a dream or a movie. The most important part, the tag line, the lesson at the end of this tale, is that I am no longer defined by Jared or my divorce. I am my own person, I am Lydia Alecia, and I am strong.

19 It feels like a drum beat

It is another beautiful morning, filled with sunshine and only a little bit of dew. We Utahans are inching ever farther from winter. The crunch of my new hiking boots is satisfying as I step out of my car. I'm more prepared this time, with a pack to hold my water and only a few essential snacks. I have a University of Colorado Mountain Lions cap on that I dug out of my old college gear, and I hope it has just the right amount of wear and tear. My hair is braided in two plaits in an effort to keep it out of my face.

Addison is the first to come up to me, and I am happy to see my new friend. She says how relieved she is that I wasn't scared away last time, and I admit to her that I'm nervous. I mentally recall the almost pathetic attempts I made this week to prepare, but after a minute of catching up with this new group, I decide to give myself a break. I did all I could in just one week, and I showed up again today. I know I won't be left behind.

Alex shows up soon after, and his smile widens when he sees me. He gives me an awkward side hug as he says hello to the rest of the group. We are still waiting for two more to arrive, so we talk about where we are headed while we wait. The views that they describe induce so much excitement in me that I am literally itching to go when the remaining members show up. I am apparently not alone, because we waste no time in leaving as soon as their feet are on the gravel.

Addison hangs back with me, and we talk easily about the sights and sounds of the world around us. She is a great hiking partner because she knows when to be quiet and soak in the surroundings and when to distract from rocky ascents with enticing conversation. The woody, natural smell of aspen trees fill my senses, and I point out that their "eyes" seem to be watching us.

Addison smiles with peace written all over her face. "I love the aspen trees here. Actually, they're what inspired me to start painting." She says this so matter-of-factly that it takes a few seconds to register. "You paint?" Her expression tells me that this activity is her passion. I need to hear more. I silently wish I had something that made me feel like she must.

Addison tells me of her first true painting: a mural of the trees where she grew up. She describes it in detail, talking of how the light shines through the high branches in the very early morning, while the forest floor remains sleepy in the dark. She tells me how she used to camp with her family. She and her brother would sneak out to see and hear the world coming alive before their parents awoke. "I wanted to add all of the details that I could remember. I can still hear the silence right before dawn every time I look at that painting. It's the only piece I plan to keep for myself."

"What other paintings have you made? What do you do with them?" Her excitement is intoxicating, and I barely notice the miles we are putting in as she talks. Addison tells me of other works of art that she has made, inspired from these very trails. She describes pottery based on fallen tree trunks or river rocks. She has made light fixtures that resemble sun beans sliding through tree branches. Addison is working to open a shop at the bottom of the Wasatch mountain range in hopes that others will love her creations as much as she has loved the experience of making them.

I realize I am smiling, though I'm envious of how she has found her calling. She points out the awe-inspiring scene that unfolded before our eyes as we pass through evergreens and to a large rocky edge. The vista this group has brought me to quite literally takes my breath away. The view is of unblemished landscape for miles and miles. The birds are calling to each other as they glide, no doubt scouting for food down below.

Alex is the first to move, taking a seat on a boulder. He opens his pack and pulls out water and a few snacks. We follow suit and replenish, mostly in silence, while we take in all that the world around us has to offer. The picnic is done family-style; everything is fair game. Too soon, the group is ready to move again.

I stand and realize in a bit of terror that my body has stiffened during our short picnic. The first few steps tell me of the blisters forming over top of the ones that were almost healed from last week. I hope no one notices, but more than that, I hope I can make it back. I trudge along and get lost in my thoughts.

I wonder what it would be like to work in a job that I loved, one that felt purposeful. I think back to only a few months ago, to before everything starting changing at work. I wasn't stressed, but I certainly wasn't fulfilled. I waiver on the edge of analyzing my career choice, but remind myself that I need to support myself. There is no use diving into something that isn't really a problem. *It's probably just jealousy*, I tell myself. I vow to be happy for Addison and to think nothing more of my job until I absolutely have to tomorrow morning.

The thumping of boot steps is soothing, and though it isn't a true rhythm with so many happening in our group at the same time, it feels like a drum beat that I can move my feet to. I am tired; this is the limit of my physical ability. I can see that the others still have all of the pep in their steps, but mine is drained. I focus on the foot steps and keeping moving forward. Without trying or even realizing it, my memory envelops me.

I am with my mother, playing in the backyard of my childhood home. There is a picnic blanket spread out and we are lying on our backs, looking up at clouds and naming what our imagination forms them into.

"There's a bunny!," I say while I laugh. I point up at a fluffy cloud that looks almost nothing like anything but a cluster of cotton balls.

"I see it!," my mom lies. "Over there," she moves her hand to the left. "That one looks like an apple pie with an 'L' cut into the top, and there is steam coming out." I giggle like the lighthearted child I am. "Oh, Mom! It does not!"

She reaches over and tickles me until we both collapse, panting and wiping the tears streaming from our joyful eyes. We roll on our backs and return to cloud watching, this time silently. After a few minutes, I keep my eyes heavenward and ask if we used to play like this with dad. Mom stays quiet for a bit longer. "No," is all she says. I am confused and wanting more. I almost never ask about my dad. When I have, my mom has always answered me, though directly and with no fluff. It bothers me, so I push. "Oh. Then," I pause. "Then what did we do?" My voice is timid and small. I'm afraid that I have upset her and this confuses me more. She sighs and answers, "Your dad had a very important job and thought that working hard for long hours was the best way to take care of us." She almost forgets to add, "but he always loved you very much."

I remember feeling guilty that I ruined such a nice afternoon. My mom didn't talk about it more, and she quickly returned to calling out outlandish descriptions for the clouds. "There's a casserole of lasagna!" "Over there is Buckingham's Palace!" "Look, I see an anteater next to a huge ant hill!"

I played and laughed along, but I couldn't stop thinking about my dad and his job. I wanted to prove that I could be just like him, but that I could stay with my mom and keep her happy too. I was too young to think about having a family of my own, but I knew I wanted to do something that would make both of my parents proud.

We exit the trail onto the gravel of the parting lot. I have never been so grateful to see my car or to know that I have flip flops waiting for me. My new boots are almost off of my feet before my car door is opened. I collapse onto my seat and kick my shoes across the lot. Addison and Alex laugh at me, but only with kind eyes. My body aches and my blisters pulse, but the simultaneous calm and joy I feel from finishing this feat fills me. I smile, laugh, and brush the mud off of my calves alongside my new friends.

On the drive home, I guzzle my water and finish my snacks as I fill Zanna and Emily in on every detail of my day. They tell me of their own weekend adventures with their families. When I hang up and realize that I am almost home, the dread of the coming work week all but takes over the high I have been riding. The hope of seeing Zanna, Emily, and my new group of friends next week is all that I can hang on to to avoid a breakdown at just the thought of more grueling days at work. Something has to give, and it has to give soon. *What* is the only question.

20 Acceleration

I am exhausted. Months ago, I was nearly overcome with fatigue from emotional strain and insomnia. Now I am struggling to fit everything I want and need to do within each day, including squeezing in time with my friends and adding some semblance of a healthy lifestyle. My eating is suffering, but I am trying so hard to not just have take out or pizza every day for every meal. Some days I succeed. Other days I barely have the energy to order dinner, let alone cook.

My new friendships and the sense of relief I get when hiking are strong enough motivators to get me to the gym or out for a walk a few times each week. Texting with Zanna and Emily along with a few coffee dates or nights out are still my lifelines. Every other waking hour is filled with work, making me feel like a zombie. I went from dreading laying in my bed to coveting the time between the sheets. I have been spread so thin that I sometimes think I fall asleep while I'm walking to bed, and I don't wake up until I am showering in the morning.

Spring turns to summer. The lengthening daylight hours are incredibly helpful to my time management, but more importantly, to my mood. I despise missing all of the sunshine while I'm trapped inside my cubbyhole of an office, especially with no true coworkers to encourage me through. The "team" that used to be my coworkers sees me as their boss, and more than that, one who they think sold them out. My manager uses me as an unfortunate workhorse who is only good for the tasks she doesn't take pleasure in.

One Monday morning in June, I decide that I was meant for more than this. Instead of the same old mad rush of answering emails and handling the supply chain, I put an "unavailable" notification on my email and set the phone to go straight to voicemail. I record a new message that tells callers I will return their messages as soon as possible within the next week. With an ounce of courage, I add that they should contact Marsha with any immediate needs.

With my door closed and silence surrounding me, I create a business plan. I sketch out ideas of how to expand to different buyers. I recommend an expanded line of appliances that would be desirable in the office as well as at home. I use the knowledge I've learned in my new role, combined with all of my past training and experiences. I add details and a timeline. I *know* this will work.

Soon, the office is dimmer and the others have shuffled out. I decide to sleep on my plans and review them with fresh eyes in the morning. Before I pack up to head home, I open my email, and with rising panic, see the unanswered email count in the high double digits. My busy message mitigated some but certainly not all of my contacts. I tell myself to answer just five emails today. I can't work all night to complete these, but having a few handled before tomorrow will help me to stay calm tonight. I scroll and chose a few to respond to.

When I'm finished with four, I see that there is one with a red exclamation point next to it. It is from Marsha, and the subject line is blank. I know that this has to be the next one that I address, but it feels like a bad idea for my mental state. My shaky finger moves my mouse to it anyhow and clicks. The one line email nearly overcomes me with annoyance.

"What are you doing?" I can't interpret her emotion from these four short words. Is she angry? Curious? Threatened? My mind spirals and I decide to talk to her in person instead of risking more room for interpretation. When I stand, my body pops in at least six different places, and I grimace as I stretch my stiff muscles. I haven't moved for hours, and my body is letting me know about it. My tired legs shuffle to Marsha's office, and the evening light filters through her expansive windows. The lights are out.

I am angered that we have now reached the point where I am working longer hours than she is. More so, I am annoyed that she had a question for me and decided to type an email and leave rather than just come and talk with me in person. My shuffle is more of a stomp as I return to my office. I haphazardly type "Let's talk tomorrow" as a reply and grab my things to get out of this gloom and doom before I lose my cool even more.

My mind spins as I make my way home, but the clear air immediately takes the edge off. My anger subsides, as does my burning desire to start a new job hunt. I pull out my phone and see a few missed messages. Zanna is excited that her daughter is officially out of diapers during the day. I text back my congratulations and throw in some suggestions of what she can do with her extra money now that she won't be giving it all to Pampers. Addison asks if I would be interested in joining her and some of the group to try zip-lining. I agree before I even know when and where.

When the next morning sun crests, I feel calm and decisive. I fill myself with a good breakfast and arrive to work a few hours before everyone else. Including Marsha. I cradle my coffee, the warmth giving me a boost as I review and edit my proposal, adding flare and style where I can. *This feels good.* I realize this is just a glimmer of the spark Addison shows when talking about her work, but it is all the encouragement I need.

My door is cracked open so I can notice when Marsha comes in. Once I see her light flick on, I grab my laptop and head to the break room. Five minutes later and armed with two fresh coffees (one with caramel creamer and a touch of sugar, the other black), I rap on Marsha's door. The coffees are precariously balanced in one hand and my computer is tucked under the other. She beckons me in.

"Good morning, Marsha," I start. My voice sounds strong and sure, though I am trembling on the inside. *I need this*, I remind myself. Marsha reaches to take the coffee from my outstretched hand. There is no thank you. I push this thought from my mind. "Can I have a few minutes of your time before you get too busy? I've been working on a project..."

"Yes, I saw your notification yesterday," Marsha says curtly, before I can even finish my sentence. She does not look pleased, but I continue anyhow.

"Right. I think you'll be happy with some ideas I've come up with." Before she can invite or dismiss me, I set my computer on her desk and start my presentation. My words are smooth and practiced, as if this has been on my mind for weeks, even months. I suppose they have. The need to succeed and evoke change temporarily drives away my nerves as I confidently show Marsha my plan to expand. My numbers are precise and correct. My proposition is exact and descriptive. This will build revenue and stop personnel cuts. The outcome is exactly what this company needs.

119

My presentation comes to a perfect close, and I silently breathe a sigh of relief. Marsha stares at me with a wan smile for a beat too long. She is tired and her weekday look has started to resemble that of the weekend. "I appreciate your dedication to our company, Lydia, but this...project...is not what you've been promoted to do." "Yes, but," I start to respond. "Leave the big picture ideas to me," Marsha says curtly. "I believe you have some emails to catch up on." Her tone is final and her eyes return to her computer. They do not return to me.

I am stunned. I can't understand why there would be no follow up questions, no excitement, no anything. The adrenaline seeps from my body, and I am struggling to complete the short walk back to my office. My eyes sting as I answer two simple emails before I realize I am of no use right now. Instead, I grab my phone and spill my woes to Alex. Rather than text back, he calls me. The gesture is not lost on me. I shut my door with my foot since standing to professionally close it feels unnecessary.

His voice is soothing. This unexpectedly breaks any remaining fortress I've built around myself and the tears flow. My frustrations pour out to him in an exhausted, delirious heap. When I finish, I feel foolish and drained. I expect Alex to tell me to suck it up, remind me that this is business, and instruct me to act like a manager or whatever position it is that I aspire to become.

He doesn't do this though. He calmly tells me that it is ok to feel how I am feeling, even if this changes from despair to anger and back again. He assures me that my feelings are valid. He tells me that I am worth fighting for. He asks what he can do to help.

This rock-like foundation he is providing helps me feel safe and supported. I am able to pull myself together so that Marsha, at least, will not see the devastation she has sown. I will do what I am asked here, but I know that my ambitions to overachieve have evaporated. Alex again lets me know that it is ok to feel this way. He also reminds me that I started early this morning, and we jointly agree that I can leave when my eight hours are up, though it will be long before all of the others. This small victory allows me to breathe a little easier. I hang up, wipe my eyes, and do my job for just a few more hours.

By Thursday, I'm ready for a break. There's nothing like feeling blatantly unappreciated that makes one ok with calling off for a long weekend.

I spend Friday lounging and catching up on some housework and television. I make time for a long walk outside and even find a book to start. I realize that it has been months, maybe longer, since I have had the attention span to focus on reading. Grief consumed me for so long, and I am now finding that I replaced my grief with work. The day of rejuvenation tells me that I am ready to finally replace both of these fillers with the real me.

Friday night brings dinner with Zanna and Emily, and they are proud of me for taking some vacation. We map out some more time to take off, with a few days for relaxation by myself and a few for excitement with the two of them. For the first time in many months, I am excited for more than just the next Saturday.

This Saturday, however, was worth waiting for. The sky is the perfect mix of sunshine and white clouds, and the air has almost no humidity in it. It is the ideal day to be outside in the forest. I have never been zip-lining before, but there is an instructor with us to keep us safe. Addison and Alex are with me, and the sheer joy emanating from each of them helps me to relax and just enjoy.

When it's my turn, I stand on the platform and hear the *click* of my safety harness. The leaves rustle gently just inches from my reach, and a warm breeze glides over my bare arms. I hear the count down from everyone behind me. "Three...Two...One!!!" I am pushed only slightly, and I lean forward to let gravity do the rest. The exhilarating rush of wind and speed take my breath away. My eyes tear with the acceleration and my hair is swept straight back. I fly over the trees, florae, and animals below me. I put my arms out wide. I feel like I am flying, and it is amazing.

When I reach the base, I realize that I have been holding my breath. I inhale deeply, and for the first time in so long, I don't feel the ball of anxiety stopping my lungs from completely refilling. I realize that sometimes you need to lose your breath in order to catch it.

21 Improvements

Beep. Beep. Beep.

The cadence of my mother's heartbeat is persistent. The too-precise *inhale-exhale* is generated by one of the many machines in this room that are keeping my mother alive. These create the soundtrack of my nights. I spend my days at work and my evenings in this hospital room. Jared says he is busy at work and barely makes an appearance. It has been this way for weeks, and the past few days have felt less and less like my mother is still here.

When we first came to this room, my mother was still part of the Hazel she once was. She made me promise to take care of myself, go to work, shower at least every other day, and eat something when I was with her. She wanted to see me eat to know that I wasn't lying. She wasn't wrong to demand this. Until the end, she wanted the best for me. When we first came, she packed books for us to read together. After only a few days, it turned into me reading to her. I continued to hold out hope until the day her lawyer informed me that I was the executrix of my mother's will. I suppose I knew I would be. Who else was there? But this formality hit me hard. It was only a matter of days until the beeps and rhythmic breathing were all that were left of the once strong woman who raised me alone.

This is the time for me to honor her. This is the time when I am the strong woman who cares for her. On this day, I sign the papers and consent to withdrawal treatment. This is when I hold her hand. This is when I let her go.

I suddenly realize I am sitting on my couch, sweating through the blankets piled on me, and staring straight ahead. I haven't watched any part of the show that is playing before me. Instead, I am daydreaming of my mother. I think of how much I miss her and how much I wish she was here. I realize that I have been on my own for far longer than I realized. I wish I had other family. I wish I had known my father.

I can't help by wonder what my life would have been like if it was more than just my mother and me growing up. Hazel was an awesome role model and caretaker, but it would have been easier on both of us to have more of a village like my friends had. My classmates had mothers and fathers and sometimes even a whole second set of step-mothers, fathers, sisters, brothers, and more. It was all so foreign to me.

Before I allow myself to feel truly lonely, I think of how my social group has grown. Zanna and Emily are basically family and have been with me for almost my whole life. Alex and Addison have grown to become fixtures for me, and it's hard to think of being without them. I breathe in, refocus my eyes on the episode of Friends in front of me, breathe out, and do my best to enjoy some rare relaxation time.

This weekend, Addison, Emily, Zanna, and I are taking a cooking class.

I am so excited for my three favorite people to be in the same room enjoying an indulgent night. We are among eight or so other people divided into three groups, each working to create a creamy Tuscan chicken dish. The spinach and tomatoes make us feel healthy, and the copious amounts of butter and heavy cream tell us that this is going to be delicious. The chef prepared rosemary garlic bread ahead of time that is now baking while we cook. The mixing aromas make us drool, and the flowing merlot makes us laugh.

This creative task brings us all together, and it is as if Addison has always been a part of our group. The chef teaches us how to set the table for a dignified dinner party. We laugh and work together to create a masterpiece worthy of a magazine centerfold. The olive colored cloth napkins with rustic brass holders adorn tiered plates and shined silver. Vine garland drapes the table runner. Our wine goblets are as full as our crystal water glasses, and candelabras fill any empty space on the linen.

Zanna brings our culinary creation to the center of our table, and Emily cuts the warm bread, fresh from the oven. I fill the dipping bowls with olive oil, and Addison adds the spices of rosemary, thyme, garlic, and anything else the chef recommends. We plan every detail of a dream trip to Tuscany and vow to eat like this more often.

Once we are seated and our plates are filled, I raise my glass to propose a toast. "Here is to my friends and the many adventures that are to come." Emily and Zanna emphatically cheer, "Hear, hear!". Addison smiles and says, "Here is to *Wasatch Wonders*, bringing a piece of Utah outdoors to everyone." She pauses before adding, "And making me a mogul entrepreneur".

"What!?," I nearly jump out of my seat. Addison smiles with a glint in her eye while she takes a sip of her wine. She sets her glass down and casually starts to serve our meal. "Stop serving and tell me what you did! Did you open your shop?," I can barely contain my excitement for her. Zanna laughs, "No, don't stop. Just talk while you serve." Addison tells us about the process of finding the perfect location for her shop, formally setting up her business, and working to complete as many art pieces as possible while still keeping the joy of creation in the process. Her sense of fulfillment is contagious, and we are beyond happy for her. The shop's opening day is next weekend. Zanna, Emily, and I promise to be there.

To commemorate the evening, we ask the chef to take our picture. It takes at least five shots to get the perfect one, but it is a keeper. We send it to Alex, who jokes that he is offended that he wasn't invited. The rest of the night is very fulfilling...in a carbs and wine kind of way!

All week at work, Marsha is acting very odd. She is more standoffish than usual and continues to only leave her office as absolutely necessary. Her blinds are drawn and the door is shut. It doesn't matter that two of her walls are made of glass; they may as well be cement.

I sigh and walk to the break room. Courtney is there sorting through coffee pod choices. I hesitate, but head in any how. "Good morning!," I say, as brightly as I dare. I don't want to seem hypocritical, but I don't want to ignore her. I know that anyone else would have made the same decision as I did when offered a promotion. Standing up to Marsha at that moment would only have gotten me, or anyone else in the situation, fired. She would have taken it as an easy out to let someone go and move on to offer the position to the next in line.

"Hey, how's it going?," Courtney responds, nicer than I expected. I shrug. "Alright." Courtney nods and then silence hangs between us. On a whim, I ask, "Would you like to get lunch today or a drink after work?" Courtney's eyes flash fear for just a fraction of a second, and it confuses me. She covers it up by turning to start her coffee, and in that moment I realize that she is afraid that I am trying to fire her. I am filled with shame. "It's ok if you're busy," I stammer. "I just thought we could catch up. Things have been," I search for the right word, "hard". She turns back and gives me a smile with just a hint of sadness. "Sure." I am more relieved than I expected. Maybe I'm not the social pariah I thought I have become. "Let's get drinks after work. Should we invite Charles?" "Definitely," I nod. Courtney tops off her coffee and gives me a warm smile. "Good luck today," she says as she heads back to her desk.

Back in my office, I feel a moment of peace, as though this might be the next step in improving the mood at work. I feel hopeful and ready to work. There is a message on my calendar of a new event scheduled for tomorrow afternoon. I open it to see it is titled "Improvements," with Marsha hosting and several upper managers who must be coming in. I search through my emails, notes, and memory, and I am sure there's nothing I should do except plan to attend. I can't shake the feeling that I'm missing something.

Back on my feet, I make the short walk to Marsha's office. Despite the impenetrable fortress she is working to make her office appear like, I knock with a purpose. There is a second's hesitation when I can almost hear her sigh and roll her eyes, and then, "Yes?". This isn't exactly the same as "come in," but I am frustrated with her games. I stroll in confidently, giving the aura of the manager she promoted me to become.

She clearly does not love this. Her hair in pinned back in a tight bun and her eyebrows have been plucked into narrow lines, giving her a cartoonish look. "Hi Marsha, I see that you added a meeting to my schedule tomorrow. What can I help you with?" I want to make it clear that I intend to be involved rather than just offer an empty request for show.

Marsha leans back in her oversized chair. Her tan pant suit and pulled-back hair make her almost blend into the wooden shelving behind her. I think I see fear on her face, though it may just be lines of exhaustion. "No, thank you Lydia. I know that you've been doing enough here." She leans forward to return to the project on her computer screen. "I'll see you tomorrow afternoon." This could have been a question, but it isn't. It is also a dismissal. I am determined to remain in control, at least of myself. "I'm looking forward to it," I say, as I stand, smooth my outfit, and walk out with my head held high.

22 Progression

Bon Jovi is singing in the background, and the tables are filling with customers around us. Courtney, Charles, and I lean in to talk to each other over the noise. It isn't bothersome noise. It is welcome, actually. I am happy to have such a normal evening out. Part of me wishes I was already in bed and sleeping, but most of me is excited to take part in the real world. Courtney and Charles seem to be in agreement.

"I'm sorry I've been so distant," I say after we finish the usual round of hellos followed by complaints about work. Their complaints are a little less specific than they were the last time we met, but I can understand why they would want to hold back. Courtney responds, "Honestly, we're surprised you wanted to catch up at all. We are also a little afraid that you're here to tell us we need to work harder or that we are getting fired."

Her direct comment stings, and I catch myself physically recoiling. "That's fair," I decide to respond. If she is brave and kind enough to be honest, I will do my best to reciprocate. "I would have thought the same thing. I'm sorry that it seems like that. It doesn't change the fact that I was the one to let Jennifer go." My voice trails. Anything I say to try to justify my role in this will seem disingenuous. "This job is hard," is all I can feebly add.

My honesty seems to be accepted. Both Courtney and Charles nod, and we all take a minute to sip our drinks and take in the surroundings. The group to my right erupts in laughter, and we all inadvertently join in. Courtney is the next to speak. She changes the subject swiftly with a detailed account of the latest show she is binge watching. I smile, take another sip, and try to enjoy the rest of the evening.

The next morning, I do my best to look the part of deserving, hardworking manager, though my heart is not completely in it. I tell myself to snap out of it. I have to play the part, even if I don't feel it, especially with today's meeting pending. I shave my legs and blow dry my hair. I pick out a knee-length pencil skirt, black with white pin stripes. I hope the sapphire silk button-down will compliment my blonde waves. In front of the floor length mirror, I add power heels and smile at the result.

I walk past Marsha's office and notice that we are back to her coming in before me. While it may not be the best business plan on my part, I am happy to think that I am doing a better job of balancing my life, even if it's just a small change. I wave at Charles and say hi to Courtney.

The morning glides by quickly, filled with an ever-increasing amount of tasks. *Ping!* A notification pops up on the bottom right of my screen, alerting me to a change in this afternoon's meeting. I open it and am frustrated to see the time has been delayed from 2:00 to

4:00. Nothing good can come from a meeting with your higher-ups in the last slot on a Friday. I work to push it from my mind and focus on my tasks.

I allow myself a few breaks throughout the afternoon to keep up with Zanna, Emily, Addison, and Alex. Tomorrow morning, I am meeting Addison, Alex, and a few others to try horseback riding. We are all nervous and excited. No one in our group has done this before, so I will finally be right on par with everyone. I smile as I think of the confidence I am building, along with a few muscles as a bonus.

Four o'clock nears, and I take a minute in the restroom to touch up my hair and make-up. Marsha walks in, presumably with the same plan, and startles a bit when she sees me. I give her my best warm smile and tell her that she looks nice today. She barely mumbles a "thank you." I walk out, not looking back. Though I hope this exuded humble confidence, I am a bit shaken and hope I did not present as cocky.

I bring a bottle of water, a note pad, and two pens to the conference room, just in case. There are three men in suits there before me, and I greet them with handshakes and what I hope is a bright smile. I am relieved to know that my outfit choice was appropriate. I seem to fit the part, and there is no suggestion, verbally or otherwise, that I do not belong here. Marsha is the last to enter. She is laser-focused on her computer and looks up only to briefly greet the three men. There is no acknowledgement to me.

Her PowerPoint displays on the screen before us, and Marsha begins her scripted thank you to us for joining her. She reviews where we were as a business the previous year. Then she goes back farther, recapping our "roots" and the progression since establishment. She continues on and points out the similarities and differences of our business models of when we were at our most productive and successful and of where we are now.

This is starting to sound very familiar.

Marsha switches gears into a plan of action. She hasn't made eye contact with me this whole time, but now, she shifts her entire body to have her back turned towards me. She fumbles over her words, but the presentation compensates for it. The plan is exact and descriptive. Marsha describes how it will build revenue and stop personnel cuts. She emphasizes that the outcome is exactly what this company needs. Her words are weak, but the graphs are strong. Her demeanor is faltering, but the facts speak for themselves. Her ending is poor, jagged, and unsure, but the bottom line is in black and white before us on the screen.

The men clap. I sit still. They congratulate Marsha on her hard work, on going above and beyond her job to develop such a sound plan, and on being a true team player. My body trembles before a cool, calm spreads over me. I ask Marsha what her inspiration was for such a committed and thorough plan. For the first time since before entering the room, her gaze lands on me. She intends it to be paralyzing. She hopes it will silence me. But it doesn't. I am rejuvenated and strong. I return her gaze while the others chime in that they, too, would like to hear more.

She holds my gaze for a moment longer, and a sinister expression pulls the corners of her lipsticked smile upwards. She turns back to her superiors and shares a heartwarming story of her dedication to our "team" and how her heart goes out to those who had to be let go, "for the betterment of the company," she is sure to add.

I press on. "Marsha, your attention to detail is impressive. I'd like to learn from you. How did you find and organize your data so effectively?" Her smile widens, but it has an alarming edge to it. "Well, Lydia, after you have spent as many years dedicated to our company, you'll understand. Maybe you'll get there one day." This last sentence was a step too far, even for Marsha. One man in a tasteful khaki suit, perfectly white button down, and a tie that happily matches the sapphire color of my top, clears his throat with just a little bit of concern. "I would like to hear this, too. Lydia, I like your willingness to learn. Thanks for asking questions." "Of course!," I smile warmly back. "I'm really interested in hearing how Marsha came up with this. It is something I want to aspire to one day."

Marsha's smile is gone, replaced by a haughty sneer. She stumbles through a description of the software than gives us our performance reports, throws in false research on our team, and adds in only partially correct data on our competitors. The others seems to buy it, though only barely. Marsha's blouse is forming small, dark circles under her arms. She takes several deep sips of her bottled water.

The same man asks Marsha for her business card. She pats her pockets and laughs nervously. "I seem to have forgotten them." "That's ok," he responds. "Can you just write your extension down in case we have any questions to follow up?" Marsha again pats her pockets and is, again, empty handed. "Here, Marsha. I have an extra pen." I hand her my pen and settle back in my chair. I am done for the day.

Marsha flatly thanks me and gives me a not-so-subtle cue to leave. I take my time saying goodbye to her bosses and carry myself as professionally out of the room as possible. Marsha shuts the door behind me.

23 White knuckles

The air is cool with clouds creating a blanket between the earth and sky. Rain is coming, but later. For now, we are enjoying a guided trail ride on horseback. We are happy to know that it is easier than we expect. My horse is named Daisy, and she is a beautiful palomino with a flowing mane nearly the same color as my own. She has a groomed, plaited tail that swishes back and forth with each step. Our group winds up a smooth, double track trail, the *clomp clomp clomp* fitting in with the rustling leaves and trill of forest insects. We ride mostly single file and in silence. It is majestic.

The trail widens and we are eventually able to walk side by side. The horses are so trained; we are just passengers along for the ride. They couple up in the ways they want, ignoring any direction we try to steer them. I find myself almost shoulder to shoulder with Alex. "I'm so glad I found you!," I say, laughing. "This is something I couldn't have imagined myself doing a year ago." Alex smiles back at me. "I don't believe that. I know you well enough now to know that you would have created some excitement for yourself. I mean, you found me *online*!". "I guess that's true. But, I'm still glad I found you." We spend the next several minutes riding along and catching up with each other.

Daisy moves in and out of the line. One minute I'm chatting with someone, and the next, I'm in the back of the pack with my own thoughts. Soon enough, Daisy lines me up with Addison. We stay in silence a bit longer. As the chatter around us picks up, I comment on the tall trees that form a canopy above us. She points out animal tracks alongside ours.

I ask her how her preparations are going for opening day, which I realize with a start is planned for tomorrow. She tells me about all of the work she has put into making the day perfect and admits that she should probably be there now. "I know I have everything set up and ready. Part of me is anxious that I'm not there double checking everything right now, but I know that this will reset me so I can have a better eye this afternoon." I agree with her and offer to not talk about it so she can enjoy the break.

"Actually, I'm glad to have the chance to talk about opening day with you. I am ready, but only for the short term. I know I can work hard enough to keep everything stocked for now, but the more I get into things, the more I know I need...I *want* someone else. I would love someone with sales experience to help me run things."

She pauses, waiting for me to respond. I can't though. My voice is caught in my throat, and I am afraid I might be misinterpreting her. "So....?," she asks. "Me?," I ask timidly. Addison continues, "It's a big ask, I know. I know you have a good job and...". "My job has been getting worse and worse. Tell me everything about this." My heart is beating, and not just because Daisy and the rest of the team start to gallop. We will have to finish our talk later.

I am laughing with white knuckles clasped on the reins. Leaning forward feels like the natural motion to avoid being thrown off, but Daisy interprets this as a cue to go faster. Adrenaline courses through me as I feel the first fat drops of rain. Before long, it is coming down in sheets and the mud from so many hooves is tossed up all over us. When we get back to the barn, the guide is wary of what our responses to such mess will be. She is immediately consoled by our laugher and the glee on each of our faces. A little rain and mud isn't enough to deter this group from a good time.

We towel off and say our goodbyes. Addison tells me she has to get back to the store and asks if I am still planning to come to opening day tomorrow. I assure her that I am, as are Alex, Emily, and Zanna, and I ask what I can do to help. She tells me that she has it under control, but asks that I come with an open mind and a little bit of time to talk business after I see the place for myself.

There is laughter above me. I open my eyes and see a broad smile looking down on me. His hand ruffles my curls, and his smooth voice beckons me to wake up. "Come on!" He turns and leaves through the open door. My legs barely reach the ground from my toddler bed. My cotton nightgown falls to my calves and keeps me warm. I run out the door after him. "Come on, pumpkin!" His voice beckons me from the hallway, and I see his slippered foot just cross into the guest room. "Daddy!," I squeal. "I'm in here!," he yells back.

The guest room is dark and empty, a stark change from the sunlight I saw pouring out of the doorway just a moment ago. There are cobwebs in every corner and a thick layer of dust on each surface. "Daddy!," I yell, but there is no joy in my voice this time. "Daddy!"

My shaky voice echos against the bare walls.

The nightmare has me confused, and I'm not sure I where I am when I awake. It takes a few long seconds to register my now familiar four walls. The clock says 7:14 in the morning. With a sigh, I roll over onto my back and stare up at the ceiling. Sunbeams are starting to come through the blinds and stripe the blank white canvas above me.

I spend the morning lounging and enjoying some of the morning news, but it isn't long before I replay my dream. I only saw a glimpse of my father in my dream. It's all I ever see because I can barely remember him. I rummage through a stack of mail, lists, and restaurant menus on my counter and find what I'm looking for.

I see Alex's young, blue eyes staring up at me. My father seems so happy and comfortable with him. I study the house behind them and morph it into the present day scene in my mind, and I wonder what my dad thought of Alex. I bet he would laugh at how he is one of my best friends now. I set the picture down and smile, thinking that Alex really is one of my best friends. I glance back at the picture and silently thank my dad for joining us.

Zanna, Emily, and I work to finalize plans for the afternoon. I'll pick them up, and then we'll stop at the store for some champagne to toast Addison. I text Alex, and ask what time he's planning to get to the store. *Whatever time you guys are!* I tell him our tentative schedule and he agrees on the time. He asks if shorts and a casual tee are ok. I assume it is, but this really isn't my thing. I relay the question to Zanna and Emily, who say it will be perfect for Addison's.

Why don't I just pick you up? There's no sense in you driving separately. I have an extra seat, and a bottle...or two...of champagne won't take up much room. Plus, this will be a good chance for Zanna and Emily to meet Alex before there are any crowds at Addison's.

Several minutes pass without an answer. We were talking back and forth so easily. I wonder why he stopped. *Or....not?* I text jokingly, trying to coerce a response. I tell myself that he is probably just getting ready and away from his phone. I mosey back to the couch to continue lounging for just a little bit longer.

Ping! It's Alex! *No, that's ok* is the entirety of is response.

I stop myself from berating him via text on such a short answer. *Oh, well let me know if you change your mind.* Then silence. His abrupt change in attitude confuses me. I decide to chalk it up to gender texting etiquette differences and stand to get myself ready.

An hour later, I am ready in skinny jeans (which fit better now that I've been more active and social), flats, and a trendy plaid shirt. I hope it is the right amount of mountain flare for *Wasatch Wonders*, while stylish enough for a Grand Opening. I snap a picture to Zanna and Emily, and they approve.

On the drive to Addison's, I fill my friends in on Marsha's plagiarism and deception at work. They are stunned, and agree that my work has reached a new low.

"What are you going to do?," Emily wonders nervously.
"There is no way I would stay at a job like that," Zanna adds in her two cents.
"But Lydia has been there for years! Maybe this is just a phase. She needs the job."
"Lydia can find a new job. She can't be used like that," Zanna says definitively.

I feel like I have an angel and devil on my shoulders, with Emily in the passenger seat and Zanna leaning against the car door in the back seat behind me. "I don't know what do to." It isn't much of an answer, but at least it stops them from bickering over it.

To change the subject, I tell them about my text exchange with Alex today. "Has he said anything since?," Emily asks. "Not a word." "That *is* really odd," Zanna says, almost to herself. Then to us she decides, "Let just wait until tonight to see how he is. I'm sure he just got busy or something." She's probably right, but something just feels off.

24 A dark cloud

Opening day is even better than I expected. Addison did a great job of marketing, and she clearly has a lot of contacts from a variety of groups. There are those from our adventuring pack, some art friends, her neighbors, friends from school, family, and many others who have wandered in after seeing the signs and advertisements tactfully scattered through every avenue available. The building itself is a perfect home for Addison's art. The walls are made of logs as if we are inside of a cabin. Her own light fixtures hang from the ceiling, doubling as product display and practicality. Her paintings line the walls and look like windows of the world around us in all four seasons and at different times of day. The piece that I am drawn to the most is a miniature sculpture of a squirrel. It is the perfect combination of realism and whimsy, and I know this is what I'll be taking home with me tonight.

Addison is busy playing host but takes a few minutes to show the three of us around. We congratulate her, and I promise to talk with her more when she has the time. I feel a tap on my shoulder. I spin around to see Alex's broad smile and bright blue eyes. He greets me with a hug and acts like nothing is wrong. *I guess Zanna was right.*

"Alex!" I hug him back. "This is Zanna, and this is Emily." He juts out his hand to offer a confident shake. "I've heard so much about you both. It's nice to finally meet you. I'm glad you've been taking care of Lydia all this time." The three ease into flowing conversation, and I realize I've talked to each of them about the others enough that they feel like they know each other. I'm relieved to see how smooth this introduction is, and I find myself hanging back and taking it all in.

At the refreshment table, the champagne we brought fits in with the others Addison has prepared. I pour myself a glass and wander around the store. I never doubted Addison, but it is an even more spectacular presentation than I expected. I can see how this could be more than she can handle on her own, especially since she is the sole supplier of her inventory.

Addison walks up beside me and tops off my glass before adding to her own. We clink our flutes and look around. "This is really amazing, Addison. You should be proud." "Thank you! I am," she says with a coy smile. "But I *am* nervous. I want to know that I can continue this for a long time, not just for a season or two."

Everyone in the shop seems to be having a good time. Alex, Zanna, and Emily are still talking away, the bell above the door sounds routinely over the soft music playing from speakers above, and there is the murmur of excited conversation from every corner. Addison puts a small sign on the counter that says "ring bell for service," and asks me to come in the back. She gives me a short description of her business plan, both for the short term and for the next five years. She tells me that if I'm interested, she will share the financials, and we can have a real conversation about working together. I only nod in agreement; I am too afraid of what I will say if I open my mouth. I can tell that she knows this though, because she laughs a little at my awed, slack-jawed expression. "Think about it," she says. She clinks her glass to mine once more, and casually returns to join the crowd. There are two people already waiting at her counter.

On the drive home, Zanna and Emily talk about Alex. They comment on how easy he is to talk with, how much he seems to have in common with me, and how kind he is. They spent the majority of the night with him in order to, as Zanna put it, "make sure he isn't a serial killer". It seems like he passed their test. They also said they picked his brain about the picture of Four Hundred Sycamore, but with no more luck than I had. We spend the rest of the ride laying out the pros and cons of Addison's offer. I am no closer to a decision when I drop my friends off.

On Monday morning, I dress while a dark cloud hangs above my head. Returning to work with Marsha is about the last thing I want to be doing. I run a brush through my waves and dress in navy blue pants and a simple, white top with small ruffles on the capped sleeves. I add my mother's pearl earrings to give me strength, and I complete the outfit with her matching pearl bracelet. Regardless of how today goes, I want to start the day by feeling good about myself. I remember the hard work that I have put into my job and remind myself that my integrity is enough to give me the courage I need. Looking the part doesn't hurt though.

There is no sense in prolonging this conversation. I will not sugarcoat it with coffee as a peace offering either. I march right into Marsha's office with only a quick, firm knock on her door. Courtney and Charles are watching me, and I don't wait for Marsha to invite me in.

"What you did on Friday was low, Marsha. I work hard for this company and for you, and I deserve better." I am being bold, but I know that I need to be. Marsha pauses, and then says softly, "You weren't promoted to do the thinking. You were promoted to do the jobs that I gave you." She has sunk lower than I expected, and I audibly gasp. She continues, "I chose you because I thought I could trust you. And then, without asking, you start your own...project...in an attempt to undermine me. I expected more from you, Lydia."

For a moment I feel guilty. Did I undermine her? Was that my goal? *No,* I tell myself firmly. Marsha is twisting my actions and trying to manipulate me. Again. "No Marsha, I was trying to help the company, our co-workers..." She cuts me off, *"Your* co-workers. My employees." Her sinister expression is showing again.

"What happened to you?," I say, harnessing my anger while noticing what Marsha has turned into. I almost feel sorry for her. "What happened? I'm doing what I need to do. I'm doing my job, and I suggest you do the same," Marsha snaps.

Then it is clear. I cannot stay here. I can't return to my previous job, I can't continue working in this position, and there is no room, or personal desire, to move up here.

"No."

"No?," Marsha asks, incredulously.

"No," I respond. "Thank you for the opportunity Marsha, but please accept my resignation." I turn to go, the anger drained but my determination steady.

"Absolutely not, Lydia. If you walk out of here, I will not accept your resignation. Instead, you will be fired!"

It's my turn for a sinister smile to curl my lips. I don't turn back. Instead, I walk out.

25 Brave

"Addison!," I nearly scream into the phone. "Hey, Lydia! Are you alright?," she answers with an edge of concern in her voice. "Yes," I think my smile is audible through the phone. "I quit my job today! Well, more accurately, I was fired." "Wait, what? How?," Addison tries to connect the dots, but I'm not really giving her enough to go on. Never mind that. There's time for details later. "It's a good thing. I did nothing wrong except outperform my boss apparently. When she retaliated, I said I quit, but she fired me instead. This means I leave on my own accord *and* I will get a severance package. When can we get together to talk more? Do you still want me to work for you?"

Addison is trying to take my fast rambling in. "Wha... Wait. That is a lot of information. Most importantly, no, I don't want you to work for me." The blood drains from my head, and I immediately feel faint. "Oh...," I say softly. "No, Lydia! I want you to work *with* me! The only way this will work is if we are a collaboration. I take the lead on the things I know, and you take the lead on the things you know. The other issues we will handle together."

What a relief! She must have heard my sigh of joy, because she laughs just a little. "I'm sorry I scared you. I have some customers

144

here now, so I can't talk. Can you come by after close?" My knee jerk reaction is that I don't have time before I have to get ready for work tomorrow, but the reality washes over me in a welcome wave. "Absolutely. Let me know if you need me to come early to help with anything while the store is still open." "That's ok, Lydia. Take some time to enjoy yourself! You probably haven't had this kind of freedom in years." She's right. *What will this new life hold for me?*, I nearly wonder out loud. We say our goodbyes, but I keep my phone out. My head is still spinning.

I plan to call Zanna and Emily on the way to the store tonight. I know the timing will be better for their schedules. Instead, I call Alex and tell him the good news. "Wow, Lydia, congratulations! You are so brave." "Brave?," I ask. "I wouldn't call it brave. I would call it out of options". "No, you had options," he assures me. "You could have stayed. You could have given up and been Marsha's yes-man...or woman. You would have hated it, but you could have stayed. Instead, you chose to stand up for yourself and for your co-workers." "Past co-workers," I remind him. "Right," Alex laughs. "But seriously, Lydia. I'm not sure I would have been able to do that. You should be proud."

Alex's words build me up, and I am thrilled at my decision. Instead of heading straight home, I walk to Jake's Café. The weekday ambiance excites me. I enjoy a delicious caramel latte and a fresh apple turnover. The flakey crust is baked to perfection. Courtney texts me to tell me she heard that I was fired. Marsha was sparse on the details, which made it clear to the others that there was more to the story. Courtney said Marsha was trying to make it look like I did something wrong, but wouldn't, or couldn't, share any details. *I know there's more to the story*, she texts. *Can I take you out for drinks tonight to congratulate you?*

Her offer to pay reminds me that I have no real income anymore, and a bit of panic rises. I make a mental note to take a deep dive into my finances, especially once I hear what my *previous* job will give me as severance. I tell Courtney that there is definitely a story but ask for a rain check on drinks. *I have plans for tonight that will hopefully lead to more good news. After that, I'll know my schedule more. Can I get back to you tomorrow?* Courtney quickly replies, *I can barely wait!*

Following suit, Alex texts me more encouragement and asks to take me out to dinner to celebrate after I meet with Addison. I sit back and feel certain that my decision was the right one. Not only am I away from the stress, negativity, and undermining that made up my previous job, but I will have a small financial safety net, a hopeful job lined up, and most importantly, a support group ready to help me celebrate. I ask Alex to save a spot for me on his calendar later this week once I have a better idea of what lies ahead. I pack up my things and take the long way home, enjoying every bit of sunshine on the way.

The parking lot of *Wasatch Wonders* is mostly empty, with only three cars. I know Addison's pine green Rogue. The Subaru with two muddy bikes on the back fits the scene, but I'm surprised at the minivan with a strip of wood paneling on the side. I chalk the diversity up to Addison's good connections and even better marketing skills.

The bell rings as I open the door, and the soft music and quiet murmuring of a few shoppers greet me. The smell of lilies combined with evergreen that Addison is using around the store takes me back to Christmas shopping with my mother. I can almost feel her presence next to me, the smell of her favorite perfume giving me a calm that I crave. I wish she was here. I know she would love this store, and I hope desperately that she would be happy for me.

"Lydia!" Addison's cheerful but hushed voice snaps me out of my reverie. I give her a hug and tell her that I will look around while the last customer checks out. Addison has the look of artist-gone-entrepreneur down. Her fitted, plain black shirt and dark blue jeans complement her dangling feather earrings. Her hair is pulled back in a neat, tight ponytail, and her make-up is tasteful. I am happy for my friend.

I am also happy to see the last customer paying for a large canvas painting that is particularly beautiful. It is one that caught my eye on opening night. Two trees flank the sides, opening to a gorgeous and very realistic vista far below. It takes me back to our hike, when we snacked on a boulder overlooking the vast openings of Utah. The man leaves with a smile on his face, and Addison locks up behind him. She is glowing. "That is the most expensive painting I had out! I need to get to work to replace it." She pauses, then lets out a deep, slow breath. "I'm so glad you're here."

We head to the back and catch up on the details of both of our days. "You are so brave, Lydia." I wince at the same description Alex used of me. "You must be kidding me. Look at how brave *you* are!" I point out the beautiful paintings, sculptures, and jewelry around us, waiting to stand in place of what was sold today. Addison smiles and nods. "We can both be brave."

The rest of the evening is filled with non-disclosure agreements, numbers, and plans written in legalese. There is definitely work to do in order to make this place last once the newness wears off, but there is potential. Addison asks me to take a few days to think about it before I officially agree to join her. I know I don't need any time at all. Addison wants me to start as an employee, and then, if we both agree, consider a 75/25 partnership to start. It could then grow into a more even split if we both want down the road.

I tell her I'm in. Addison asks me to take a few days anyhow, even if it just means putting my feet up and resetting. She tells me that she will set up a time to meet with her lawyer so we can make things official later this week. "No hard feelings if you back out, Lydia." I open my mouth to assure her that I won't, but she adds, "Seriously. This is important for both of us. No hard feelings." I reach out my hand to hers to shake on the pact.

In the parking lot before I leave, I text Alex to ask if Wednesday or Thursday would be good for dinner. I tell him the evening with Addison went better than expected and that I will fill him in on all that I can when I see him. He agrees to Thursday and says he will send some restaurant options. *It's on me!*, he assures me. I wonder if Alex and Courtney are offering to treat because I'm out of a job or simply to celebrate.

Would it be ok to come back to my place after?, Alex asks.

The text feels odd. Is this a date? I want to think my reply through, but then I remember how his long hesitation made me feel a few days earlier. Still, this catches me off guard. I'm not sure I'm ready to date. Even if I was, I'm not sure I feel that way about Alex.

I decide to agree. I can always lay it out during dinner if it starts to feel like a date. *Sure*, is all I can think to reply. Alex sends a thumbs up, and the conversation ends. I'm left with a mixture of feelings that include elation and confusion for the rest of the drive home.

26 A woman alone at night can never be too safe

The next few days are blissfully calm. I sleep as much as possible, embracing the fact that I am actually able to sleep. I also spend as much time outdoors as I can. The fresh air grounds me, and the forward movement of going for walks helps me to mentally prepare for what lies ahead. I keep my promise to Addison and take a few days, but there are no moments of hesitation for me. I am excited about work for the first time in as long as I can remember.

Emily and Zanna are able to take a long lunch, and there is so much for us to catch up on. They are both happy for me, and while Emily wants to be sure I'm making smart financial decisions, we all feel sure that things are moving in the right direction. I am grateful for such trustworthy friends. There aren't many people with whom you can share the nitty gritty of your savings and expenses with, but I can do this with no awkwardness with these two. We look at everything and decide that I can live in the same manner that I am now for six months with no extra income. The severance package was a godsend, and while the last few months at my old job were awful, I am thankful for the savings I could amass.

Courtney and Charles meet me for drinks after work on Wednesday.

They tell me how the rumors have been flying. "Did you really call her bosses to tell them how awful she's been?," Courtney asks, eyes wide with a thirst for gossip. "No!," I laugh. "I would have liked to, but I didn't think it was necessary. Plus, I just wanted to get out of there." "Did you really call her a coward to her face?," Charles asks, equally hungry for information. "What? No! Where are you guys getting this from?," I ask. I choose to assume these exaggerations are wishful thinking on my old coworkers' parts rather than slander from Marsha. "What about the part where Marsha stole your presentation? Is that true?" Courtney is eager to know the whole story.

"Yes, that part is unfortunately true, and it was the last straw." I satisfy their need for information and tell them the whole story, down to the email from Marsha asking what I was doing and the last minute change of the meeting time so I wouldn't be able to stay and argue.

They sit back, apparently satisfied with the tale I've spun for them. "I wish I could have seen the look on Marsha's face when you asked her to explain her presentation," Charles says. "She was not pleased with me," I laugh, thinking back.

They tell me that Marsha has been in a terrible mood since I left. All of my work has been dumped on her while she is also trying to put "her" proposal into action. Charles and Courtney wear their anxiety like a coat, visible over everything. I am relieved to be away from this. They split our tab and we hug as we promise to stay in touch. I know this is unlikely.

By Thursday morning, I am ready to commit to working with Addison. She is overjoyed and has already scheduled an appointment for us to meet with the business' lawyer. She is as ready as I am. We cross the t's and dot the i's, and by the end of the night, I am officially an employee of *Wasatch Wonders*. Addison adds to the excitement by handing me a catalog of office supplies. She wants me to pick out a new laptop to have for my start date, a week from Monday, so I can work from home when needed.

Addison isn't able to stay long; she needs to head back to work. The timing is perfect, and I text Alex that it is official.

Congratulations! It's time to celebrate. Did you decide on a restaurant?, Alex texts.
Yes! Tony's Taqueria sounds delicious!, I respond.

We confirm the time and address. I have a little bit of time to kill, so I go for a drive. The sun is out and there are only a few clouds in the sky. Since it is the afternoon on a weekday, the lanes are fairly empty. The open roads and clear air welcome me, and soon I am singing along to an old Eagles song, loudly and probably out of key.

We may lose, and we may win
Though we will never be here again
So open up, I'm climbin' in

I instinctively turn my blinker on and head into a neighborhood. I slow as I realize where my subconscious has taken me. I put the car in park and look over at Four Hundred Sycamore.

The house is the same as when Alex and I were here, though the weather is even better for a walk around the neighborhood. The windows are dark and there are no cars in the driveway. I take some time looking around as if walking these roads is something I do every weekday. There are no answers to be found here, but the memory of my father is ever so slightly more solid just knowing that he was here

151

at one point. I have so little of him left. I suppose this is almost the same as visiting my mother's gravesite. It allows me to feel close to him.

Pulling into Tony's Taqueria is all I need to do to know that I've made the right restaurant choice. The smell of cilantro greets me, and my stomach responds with a growl. I guess I forgot to eat lunch today with all of the excitement going on.

Alex's Jeep is already in the lot, a smattering of mud across each side. I'm not sure I have seen his car clean yet. He is waiting for me at the door, comfortably dressed in khaki shorts, a plain green t-shirt, and Birkenstocks. The casual look relieves me, suggesting it isn't a date and allowing me to feel more relaxed in my shorts and baseball tee. He greets me with a bear hug, picks me up, and spins me around. It catches me off guard and I snort with laughter. This makes us both laugh more.

"I am so excited for you! You are going to love this place. It has the best tacos north of the border," Alex is grinning from ear to ear, and I think it's more for the food than it is for celebrating with me. "You have no idea how ready I am," I say as I follow him to the hostess.

We order enough food for a whole family. I ask for fish tacos with avocado and purple cabbage, carnitas with Mexican slaw, and a standard beef taco with hot sauce. Alex applauds my choices and orders three tacos of his own creation, showing off how many times he has been here before. We get a quesadilla, chips and salsa, and guacamole for the table. We top it off with two margaritas to make the celebration complete.

The food is as messy as it is incredible. The margaritas prove to be an excellent conversational lubricant, and we talk and laugh easily all through dinner. I forget my concerns about Alex's intentions and allow myself to relax and have fun. It is like we have been friends for years, separated only by a technicality.

When our stomachs are so full that we can almost see the food inside, we decide it's time to call it a night. The restaurant is steadily getting more crowded, and our table is in demand. Alex pays the bill as promised, and we walk to our cars. Once our feet hit the gravel of the parking lot, Alex's demeanor changes. He is nervous and awkward. I know that he is remembering his request to go to his house.

"Do you want to ride with me? I can bring you back here when you're ready to go home," Alex mumbles. I realize he has been rehearsing this. It makes me more nervous.
"Oh. No, thank you. I think it will be easier for me to take my car if that's ok." I trust Alex, but I don't like the idea of feeling trapped.
"Yeah, of course. That's makes sense." Again, he is uncomfortable and stammering.

Alex gives me the address just in case, but tells me he will be sure I can follow him the whole way. I assure him I will be fine. We separate, and I walk back to my car.

After I punch the information into the GPS, I quickly call Zanna and Emily. I tell them that I will fill them in on the rest of the day, but describe to them Alex's change in attitude as soon as we left the restaurant. "Do you feel safe?," Emily asks. "I do, but it feels weird. Do you think this is a date?" Zanna chimes in, "Yes, absolutely! Most guys would be nervous for this part. Are you sure you want to go through with it?" I think about it, and tell them that I do. "It has been so great being friends with him. I want to give him the benefit of the doubt. If it's not what I expect, I'll just leave." We chat a little more and end the call, but only after I promise to share my location with them as soon as I get to Alex's house. It seems like overkill, but a woman alone at night can never be too safe.

We pull up to a modern two-story house that appears to be cream colored, though it's hard to tell in the dark. The neighborhood seems safe, with wide streets and lights on every corner. We park in the long driveway, and before I get out, I send my location to Zanna and Emily. Alex and I walk together up his winding sidewalk, mostly in silence. I am impressed at the well-kept lawn and manicured flower beds in front.

There are already lights on in the house, and it occurred to me that I never really asked if Alex lived alone. I wonder if he has a roommate, or possibly a girlfriend. Either way, I'm surprised he wouldn't have mentioned someone. Then I remind myself that we really haven't known each other for too long. "You have a great house," I say to ease the tension with a compliment. "Thank you. My dad is big on curb appeal, so he helps me a lot." He unlocks the door and we walk in, taking off our shoes at the welcome mat.

Alex's home is neat, but clearly inhabited by a bachelor. There are very few decorations on the wall. I ask to use the bathroom, and the seat has been left up. I send Zanna and Emily a quick text to say that I'm inside and that it is still awkward. I take a minute in the mirror to freshen up. When I open the door, Alex beckons me from the kitchen. "Do you want a drink?," he asks. "I have a few Blue Moons, a few bottles of wine, and some vodka if you want something stronger." He laughs at his joke, and looks away quickly. "I'll just have a water. I'll have to get going soon." I figure I should start the process of leaving now so I have an out when I'm ready. And I am almost ready.

Alex fills a glass from the fridge and pours himself a shot of vodka on the rocks. He take a surprisingly long drink from his glass before handing me mine. He seems to steel himself before he speaks.

"I haven't been completely honest with you Lydia." I instinctively reach for my phone and take a step to the door. "No, it's nothing like that. I don't mean to scare you."

"Ok," I respond, hesitantly.

"I should have told you from the beginning, but I just didn't know how. Actually, I didn't even want to at first. You were a stranger on the internet." Alex runs his hands through his hair.

"What are you saying, Alex?" I'm nervous. My phone is in my hand, just in case.

"Once we got to know each other better, I didn't want to lose you. I hope I don't now. But it's important that I'm honest. You deserve to know."

"Alex, you're scaring me. What's going on?"

"I'm sorry. I don't mean to scare you! It's nothing like that. Just..." He hesitates again. Alex waves down the hallway and I hear footsteps.

My mind races. Have I been fooled into trusting him? I grab my phone and get ready to dial...Emily? 911? I'm not sure. Before I can decide, a man joins us in the kitchen.

His hair is sandy blonde with a bit of wave, though speckled with more grey than the last time I saw it. His eyes are a familiar shade of green.

"Hi Lydia," he says.

27 A right to be worried

The room spins and my ears feel like someone put earmuffs over them. The thump of my heart is so loud, I am deafened to everything else. I blink my eyes to refocus and grab ahold of the counter top in front of me. Alex runs over to steady me, but I shake him off. Suddenly, my senses return and become laser sharp. I see the fear in the eyes of the two men in front of me, hear their breath as they work to keep them steady, and taste the bile that is rising in my throat. I grab my keys and head to the door.

"Lydia wait!," Alex cries.

"Why? So you can con me more? I trusted you, and now you bring this man here to talk to me? Did you find him online, too? Did you post the picture to find a look alike?" I am so angry that I can barely think straight.

"No, Lydia, he isn't just a look alike."

What is that glint in his eyes? A tear? It angers me more. "My father is dead." I walk out the door and don't look back. Alex's footsteps start to follow me, but then the other voice, the calm, sad voice that I

heard just a few moments earlier, calls out to stop him. "No, Alex. Let her go. She needs time."
This man doesn't know what I need. He doesn't know me at all. I punch the gas pedal, and the car responds on cue. Soon, I am staring down headlights as I race along the highway. It isn't until these lights start to blur that I realize I am crying. I know what Alex is suggesting and what this stranger wants me to think. I'm not stupid. But it isn't possible. My mother wouldn't have lied to me. My father is dead.

My phone has been alerting all night with text messages and phone calls. I haven't looked at a single one, and I don't intend to. Instead, I set my phone to silent. I kick off my shoes as soon as I get home and leave them at the door. My clothes are strewn across the floor, a breadcrumb trail to show me how to escape this wretched apartment. It feels like it is smaller than ever and still closing in. I don't put pajamas on. I don't need to brush my teeth. There is no energy to wash my face. I crawl in bed, pull the covers over every inch of me, and do my best to shut out the world.

When I wake in the morning, I feel like I've been hit by a bus. I'm confused, and my head is pounding. A night filled with disjointed dreams that slip away faster than I can recall them has left me temporarily lost. But then I remember all of it. And I am angry.

I know I will have messages on my phone, and I know that I should talk with Emily and Zanna. But I'm not ready. I rub my eyes and look at the smudged mascara that is now on my hands. I stumble into the shower and work to scrub the night away.

BANG BANG BANG

It takes a second to realize the sound is coming the from door rather than my head.

BANG BANG BANG

It is loud enough that I decide not to ignore it, though I want to. I think whoever this is may break down the door soon.

BANG BANG BANG

I shut off the water and wrap in a towel. Water lines the pathway that my clothes left last night. "I'm coming!," I yell. I would let a murderer in at this point if it means the banging would stop. I clutch the towel to my dripping body and struggle to unlock the door. Addison, Zanna, and Emily are all on the other side. They nearly push me over on their way in. Emily pulls me into a hug. "Thank goodness you're ok! We didn't know what happened to you last night!" Before I can answer, Addison says, "Alex called me. Are you ok?"

I look at her, and then to Emily and Zanna. They look terrified and worried, though Zanna's face almost looks like she is holding back laughter. Then I realize what I must look like. I walk to the mirror and see soap through my hair and mascara running down my face. "Wow," I say, mostly to myself. "I'm fine. Let me finish my shower." I walk back to the shower and realize my words were gruff. I'm not ready to play nice yet. I still need a minute to wake up. My eye catches the clock on the way back to the bathroom. 11:52. *Alright, I think to myself, maybe they have a right to be worried.*

Fifteen minutes later, I'm a tiny bit more presentable. There is no more soap or mascara on my body, and I'm dry and wearing the first t-shirt and shorts that I found. In that measly 15 minutes, my friends have coffee ready, a pizza in the oven, and most of my dishes washed and put away. "I'm sorry for being rude earlier. I'm a little groggy."

Emily is the first to talk. "You are allowed be to be rude, groggy, or anything else that you're feeling, but you are not allowed to disappear from the face of the earth when we think you might not be safe." I look at my phone and see 37 unopened messages. It's a new record for me. "I'm really sorry. I wasn't thinking straight. Last night was a mess." I fill my mug and top off the others'. I hope playing host will grant me some grace.

"I can't believe he would do this to you. How can someone's father not contact them for 25 years?" Zanna is direct, and Emily gives her the side eye. "He isn't my father," I say before anyone else can chime in. This silences them for a few moments.

"But Lydia," Addison starts but doesn't finish. "He isn't my father. My father is dead," I say. "Ok," says Emily. "Ok. Let's just have something to eat. We are just glad to know you're safe." I move to sit down, and I realize right then that I am starving. "So we just aren't going to talk about this?," Zanna asks, stunned. "Not until Lydia is ready. Really, Zanna, you can be so insensitive." Emily takes charge, as usual, and starts to set plates and napkins out. The four of us eat pizza and honor the pretense that it is like any other day.

The week goes by in a blur. My phone has more missed messages than ever before. Zanna, Emily, and Addison take turns dropping by to check on me. They bring me dinners and make sure I'm taking care of myself. I am not. My mind wants to process what is happening, but my body refuses to let me. I am numb.

On the eve of my first day at my new job, I muster up the energy to get ready. I don't want to let Addison down, regardless of what is happening in my life. The promise of something else to occupy my mind provides some comfort, though minimal. I pack a peanut butter and jelly sandwich with apple slices. I know I won't be able to stomach this tomorrow, but I will at least try. I pick out dark jeans, tan flats, and a simple, puce top. I lay out a necklace and earrings that I hope will present as artsy but professional, and I mentally prepare a wavy pony tail to emulate Addison's look when she is working.

I collapse back on the couch and pull my blankets over me. The weight is comforting. I grab my phone and search "Alex Burke, Utah." I know Zanna did this before when we were out to dinner in what feels like a lifetime ago. Just like that night, there are no results from the search. I assume Alex has a different last name, but I really don't know. I was so eager for answers and an escape that I didn't ask many questions. I blindly fell into this trap.

My conscience pricks at this thought. Alex has been good to me *and* for me. I feel so conflicted. With a sigh and a growing knot in my chest, I open my text messages. I have so many unread messages from Alex since I silenced his conversation to stop the alerts. I steel myself like Alex did at his house and scroll up to where the unread messages begin.

There are so many "I'm sorry" and "Please let me explain" texts. Again, I am conflicted. I feel annoyed and angry at his measly attempt to reconcile, but I also feel guilty, knowing this is the only avenue for communication I've allowed him. He hasn't given up.

As the messages continue, they get longer and more informative.

I wanted to tell you from the beginning, Lydia. But please try to understand. This was a shock to me, too! He should have told me anyhow.

I had to be sure. I couldn't tell you until I knew. To do that, I had to get used to this idea, too. I could have worked with him to get used to this.

Confronting my dad was so unbelievably hard.
Our dad.

I close my messages, set my alarm, and turn on the television. I am desperate for the love saga of Ross and Rachel in reruns to capture my attention and help me to sleep.

28 The olive branch

Wasatch Wonders is a beautiful haven. The art and nature surroundings keep me calm and have the almost magical ability to enfold me inside. I man the register and restock the shelves as Addison crafts in the back. She does the budget and pays the bills. For the past few weeks, my project has been to review and improve our marketing strategies. My new laptop allows this to progress much more smoothly than it would have been before. My mind is occupied by steady, unemotional tasks, and my interactions are minimal. I am able to feel productive without stress or without needing my mind to stray too far.

"Hey Lydia," Addison says, interrupting my one-track mind on restocking some jewelry. Addison's ability to quickly produce necklaces, rings, earrings, and bracelets of colors reflecting the Utah landscape amazes me, but her added touch in making each piece unique is what makes her a true artist. There is a story, an inspiration, behind each one. I find that I restock this area frequently because they are popular amongst our customers, and I find it soothing to look at each tiny work of art.

"Some of us are going hiking this weekend. Will you come?" Addison has invited me to an event at least once each week since I started here. They have gone hiking, mountain biking, caving, and even hot air ballooning once. Addison sometimes asks me to lunch, offering to close the store just to get me out in the real world. I always politely decline. I am content just as I am. The store has been doing very well, and we both know that we need to keep working hard to succeed after the initial newness wears off. I also know that I need to put more heart into my part of the work, but that will come. I hope.

"I could really use your help," Addison continues. "I'd like to start planning for the winter line, even though it feels crazy to think that far ahead. I'd love your opinion to see if anything sticks out as an inspiration." I smile at Addison, who has been so wonderful and important to me. I don't want to let her down, but I am just not ready.

"You're the one with the artistic eye. I know you will find something perfect to be your muse. Besides, I have plans. Thank you, though." It's only a small lie. I *do* have plans, but they involve myself, some blankets, and a new book. Until recently, I haven't been able to focus on reading. My mind would stray from work to Jared to my mother and back. I was able to get some focus back before, but now, it's like I can't help but to escape into alternate realities. I set my phone to silent each night and weekend and hungrily turn page after page as if I'm making up for lost time.

"Ok," Addison says, clearly disappointed. "I hope you'll come soon. I miss you." She walks away before I can say anything. I'm grateful for her retreat through, because I have no idea what to say. The guilt of letting my friend down weighs on me, but how could I go somewhere with Alex after he lied to me? It was a gargantuan lie, bigger than I can handle. And how can I expect Addison to chose to stay with me rather than Alex, someone who has been in her life long before he entered mine. The thought creeps in, *He has been in my life since I was born. I just didn't know it.* I turn back to the jewelry section and methodically restock.

Back at the register, I wear a genuine smile onto my face. The customer in front of me is paying for a beautiful chandelier that Addison made from a fallen birch tree and then sanded into a perch for lighting. She expertly added wires and hid them under wood sculpting, allowing for farmhouse-style light bulbs to adorn five not-quite-balanced branches. The bulbs, of course, add the balance and make this a true masterpiece.

The price is high, but it is well worth it. The transaction adds to our already successful day. My phone pings to alert of a new message. Because the store is now empty, I reach for the phone to see a message from Zanna. It is not to our ongoing group chat, but sent only to me. *It wouldn't kill you to spend some time with Addison. She isn't the one who lied to you.* The honesty stings. For the second time today, I feel guilt rising up inside me.

I don't answer yet, but potential responses swirl through my mind. I know that Zanna is right. Her blunt text reminds me that I am lucky to have friends who will give me space but also tell me how it is. I am not ready to visit or talk with Alex, and I'm not sure I will ever be, but I know that I should try harder with Addison, Zanna, and Emily.

As if on cue, Addison walks out from the back to make a loop around the store. She likes to take breaks to stand and stretch, and she wants the chance for customers to see her involved in the day-to-day workings of her shop. There is no one else here though, so she turns to head back to her studio.

"Addison!," I say, almost too eagerly. It's like I am out of practice with being human. "I, um. Someone just bought your birch chandelier. She was really excited. It is truly a work of art. I bet she tells all of her friends to come here." Addison takes the olive branch that I have so clumsily and pathetically offered. Her face lights up, and she looks to where the light fixture once hung. "You're kidding! I priced that a littler higher than I thought I should, mostly because I didn't want to see it go. I'm so happy it did, though! Tell me about the person who bought it."

I love this about Addison. She not only puts her all into her craft, but she loves to know about the new owner with whom each piece connects. She says it helps her give life to more creations. I do my best to paint the picture of the lady in a sleeveless, black turtle neck, a fashion choice that has always confused me. I tell of her grey spiked hair and smart heels that compliment her professional looking make-up. Addison nearly squeals. "This is exactly the type of person I pictured when I was making it! I hope something on our hike sticks out to me to inspire a new piece to replace it." And just like that, the guilt is back.

"Addison, I'm sorry I'm not ready to hike with you. I will be one day, I hope." Addison's eyes soften. I offer another olive branch: "Can we plan something with Zanna and Emily this weekend? Maybe a picnic or bowling or something." Addison's face brightens. "Yes! Saturday evening? I'll plan something." She scurries away to plan and create, probably at the same time, obviously leaving before I have a chance to change my mind.

The bell on the door rings as an older couple enters. The man's face lights up as he sees the end table that Addison finished last week combining two distinct colors of wood in a pattern that looks like a flowing stream. The woman heads straight to the scarves, running a colorful one that accurately depicts a late summer sunset through her fingers. I push down the spike of panic that comes along with making plans after being a recluse for weeks. "Hello," I say in my best cheery voice. "I'm so glad you're here. Let me know if you have any questions or if you'd like to meet the artist, Addison." Customers seem to love this extra line I added in recently. To know that the one who made all of the beauty that lays before them is only a room away, probably creating more fantastic pieces, seems to add something to their shopping experience. They don't often accept the offer, but just knowing is enough. They begin their excited browsing, and I make a mental note to be a better friend and talk with Zanna and Emily tonight.

At home, I find myself heading to my usual spot where my blankets and half-read book await. I stop myself tonight and take just a few minutes to boil some water for tea and to text my friends. I start with a direct message to Zanna. *You're right. I'm a jerk. I'll do better.* To our group chat, which now includes Addison, I type, *Saturday evening plans?*

I'm not surprised to know that these three have been scheming already. Zanna's private response is first: *We're all jerks sometimes.* I smile. No apologies and no excuses. Just a chance to move on. Addison is next to reply to everyone. *Dinner at 7 and then bowling after? Lydia's suggestions.* We continue to plan for the weekend. I make a camomile tea that I hope will help to maintain the calm I am feeling. The rest of the night is spent exploring the Seven Seas with Peter Freuchen.

Getting ready for Saturday dinner brings a new round of nerves. I am feeling the effects of hiding in my apartment any time I am not working. I talk myself through each step of prepping, from getting into the shower through putting on my sandals.

When I arrive, I am relieved to see my friends already at the restaurant waiting for our table. Emily is in a sundress, striped in blue and white. Zanna wears jean shorts and a plain black fitted top. Addison is outdoorsy in her khaki shorts and baseball tee. They pull me into a hug, each in turn. I tell them about my anxieties getting ready for the night while trying to assure them I am happy to be with them.

"It makes sense," Emily says to comfort me. "The last time you went out, something major and life-altering happened. You're probably nervous it will happen again." This realization strikes me as true, and being able to identify the stressor helps me to relax. Zanna's name is called by the hostess and we follow her to our booth. The lighting is dim from the lamp overhead that was probably installed in the late '90s. We order drinks and quickly return to why we are here tonight.

For the first time, I am able to share the whole story of what happened that night at Alex's. Revisiting the scene in my head is painful, but I know that my friends need to hear it. I share the comfortable fun that we had over tacos earlier in the night, the awkward request to drive together, and all about Alex's house. I tell them how the man who he believes is my father must have been in the back room the whole time, listening.

"And you haven't talked to him since?," Zanna asks.

"No. I can't bring myself to. I circle between full blown anger to sympathy to confusion and everywhere in between. I just feel so misled," I confide.

"You know," Addison starts hesitantly, "Alex is a good guy. This must be hard for him too." She flinches as soon as the words are out of her mouth and prepares for my backlash. The waiter brings our drinks, his timing as inopportune as possible. He starts to ask if we are ready to order, but Zanna shoos him away with barely a glance in his

167

direction.

"But he knew long before I did, and he kept talking with me as if nothing had changed. How can you know something that enormous and keep it to yourself?," I argue my side. "Well, I know it's not the same thing, but…," Emily starts, then seems to regret it. "But what?," I implore. "It's not the same thing," she repeats, "but you knew you were going to fire that one employee at your old job. Instead of giving her a heads up, you built her trust in you and had her train her own replacement."

Ouch. That one stung. I physically recoil. I want to fight and tell her this is a completely different situation. This is a family affair and that was business. But it isn't completely different. It is deception and self-preservation, whether it was right or wrong.

"I'm sorry, Lydia," Emily continues after my silence and reflection. "You know we don't judge you for that, or for any of this. We probably all would have made the same decisions. But it might help you to look at this from a different angle." The waiter returns and Zanna nearly bites his head off. Addison breaks the tension by laughing, "I don't think he will be back anytime soon."

"Maybe I should at least try to hear Alex out," I concede meekly. "Just think about it," Emily says. Her tone is gentle and loving. "I think it would help you both." "Right," is all I can say. Addison puts her hand on mine for comfort and then hands me a menu. "Let's figure out what we want before our waiter comes back and Zanna actually stabs him." We laugh uncomfortably, and then ease into the rest of our evening together, blissfully drama free.

29 It feels purposeful

"I said *maybe* I should try to hear Alex out. I didn't say I would do it," I whine to Addison when I still haven't answered his requests in over a week. She rolls her eyes and shakes her head. We are working together to revamp one corner of the store. Our aim is to build off of the log cabin feel and make the back corner look like a living room. An overstuffed couch the color of slate sits invitingly in front of a DIY fireplace. The flames aren't real but rather are created from pieces of red, gold, and black jewelry, each lovingly made by Addison. A hand-stitched throw made of vibrant yarn from native sheep drapes over a burned orange ottoman.

"It's time, Lydia. This has gone on too long, and it's taking its toll on you and on Alex. You don't have to decide what to do next or who you want in your life right now, but you do need to hear the story. It isn't healthy to ignore your past."

Addison is right, of course. Despite coming out of my shell with Zanna, Emily, and Addison, I have continued to draw inward. I feel safer at home or at the shop than anywhere else, despite how much I sometimes despise my apartment. I am prepared for what will happen when I stay home. Nothing. That's what will happen. This, I know, is not healthy. Addison points it out now, but I am already aware.

"I will. I promise. Soon." It's the best I can do. "Then come this weekend. We are going for a long, easy bike ride. You will have plenty of people and scenery to keep you occupied so you can ease into it with Alex," Addison nearly pleads. "Next time." I turn my eyes to the lampshades painted like the night sky that I am displaying over dimly lit bulbs in our faux-house. Addison sighs and returns to fluffing and rearranging the many pillows on the couch.

My weekend plans include my couch, a cup-o-noodles (or two), and The Hunger Games trilogy. Laundry is piled high and groceries are running low, but I am content to stay where I am, cozied up with my favorite blanket and a stack of soft pillows. Katniss Everdeen rides the train to the Capitol while Peeta strategizes with Haymitch. I follow along with unabashed enthrallment, noodles being slurped noisily.

My phone rings, and I see that it is Addison. I press ignore so I can learn more about Cinna's heartfelt conversation when meeting the heroine. The *ping* signals a voicemail that I forget about almost as soon as it sounds. Not five seconds later, the text alert sounds. I shut my phone off completely so I can focus on the saga unfolding in the words in front of me and coming to life in my imagination.

A small *thud* makes me jump, and I realize that after reading more than 250 pages without a break, my eyes had given up and I must have fallen asleep. I grab the piece of mail substituting for a bookmark and flip through the now-closed novel to find the last place I remember reading. I'm sure I read more, but whether or not I was awake when I did it is up for debate.

My knees pop in protest as I unfold myself and attempt to move out of the pretzel shape I formed with my body hours before. I stand to stretch and hear more creeks and cracks than a body my age should produce. I grab my phone to check the time and remember hazily that I had turned it off. I was so focused on my alternate reality that I completely forgot about Addison's missed call.

The phone powers up almost as slowly as I am moving. It seems to have noticed the happy snail's pace today is taking. I refill my mug with steaming tea and walk around the kitchen to stretch my legs. It only takes about four steps in each direction, but my legs are grateful.

My phone lights up with full power and immediately starts to vibrate for a solid minute with missed messages. *What now?* I roll my eyes and mosey over to the phone to begin the process of prioritizing. I assume some will be from Alex, renewed energy from this morning's ride to fuel his apologies.

There are none from Alex, which surprises me. I have three voicemails from Addison, one from a number I don't recognize, and about 15 texts from my other friends. I decide to jump into the missed texts first. Addison's most recent message contains only capital letters. *CALL ME.* The preceding messages paint an ominous picture. *Why aren't you answering?* and *Where are you?* sum up her pleas.

I see no reason to listen to the voicemails. That would only waste time and elicit more questions. I dial Addison. It rings six times and goes to voicemail. My heart's beating may as well be a bass drum, it is so loud. I flip back to my messages and see that both Emily and Zanna are wondering where I am, too. I can almost hear Emily saying "You're not allowed to disappear from the face of the Earth…" just a few weeks prior as the four of us sat around my kitchen table.

They are not my mother and don't need to know my every whereabouts, but I do seem to go missing or silent when something major happens. My foggy daydreaming is interrupted by my phone's intense vibrations. I nearly drop my phone in its insistence in being noticed. It is Addison. I take a deep breath and answer. "Hello?" The word is barely out of my mouth before Addison starts talking. "Lydia. Thank goodness. Why haven't you been answering?!" Her focus on me gives me a moment of relief. This must just be because I didn't answer my phone again. *Thank goodness.* But then she continues. "Lydia, there's been an accident. It's Alex. He was hit by a car during our bike ride this morning."

The world tips and fades to black. My shaky hands reach out to find something, anything, to hold on to as my knees buckle and give out. For the second time in just a few minutes, my thunderous heartbeats drown out all other sounds. "Lydia? Lydia?!" Addison's voice beckons to bring me back. I'm not sure that I want to come back though. But it isn't my choice. The second I can control my thoughts enough to know I don't want to return to reality, my vision corrects and my heart, still pounding, lessens ever so slightly in volume.

"I'm here," I manage to say. "What happened? Where is he? Is he....?" The word on the tip of my tongue tastes like ash and causes bile to rise up. I am not able to voice it.

"He is at the medical center in Ogden. You need to get here. Soon."

I tell her I will, and she promises to text the details of where to go. I am thankful, because I wouldn't be able to remember in even one minute with how my mind is swirling right now. I grab a bag and throw in whatever I think might be necessary, though who even knows what is necessary in a time like this. I have a change of clothes that probably doesn't match, a toothbrush, my phone charger, and a handful of snacks. I figure I can buy anything else that I need at the hospital. As I almost trip over my not-yet-fully-on shoes at the door, I remember something that might help. I'm not sure why I think this, but I do. I run to my bedroom and grab the picture of Alex and my dad from so many years ago.

I take just one extra moment to look, really look, at the two staring back at me. I hope that I will be able to see those eyes again. Both sets.

I grab my keys and fly down to the street. My feet barely touch the ground. Once I'm in my car, I force myself to sit and breathe deeply for a few seconds. It will not help if I get into an accident on the way to the hospital. I look in the mirror and wish I had put on make-up this morning, or at least that I had brushed my hair. My appearance reminds me of college girls who roll into their morning classes in sweats and a nest of hair pulled into a bun right on top of their heads. It's no matter. I just need to get to the hospital.

The drive goes as smoothly as can be expected. Every stoplight causes a slew of profanity to escape my mouth, and all of the drivers on the road seem to be extra diligent with following the speed limit. It is stressful, but there are no accidents or major traffic jams, and I am grateful.

The hospital parking garage greets me ominously. Lights at the entryway are burned out except for one remaining light flickering. I hear the *buzz buzz* as the nearly exhausted bulb tries to stay alive. It feels purposeful, like a bad omen. I shake the thought from my mind and pull in to the first spot I see. Only when I near the emergency room doors on foot does it occur to me that I should have written down where I parked. I will never find my car now, but that is a problem for another time.

173

The doors to the vestibule *swish* open and the sudden rush of silence takes me off guard. I envisioned a *Grey's Anatomy*-esque pit with doctors running around and into their coworkers, yelling for pints of blood and shouting, "Clear!". The confusion must have shown on my face, because a kindly older women with a hospital badge touches my arm. "How can I help you, dear?," she asks. Her blue eyes shine with age and wisdom as she asks this unilateral question. She wants nothing in return, only to help me. I pray that she, anyone, can help Alex.

I fumble with my phone to pull out the message from Addison. My mouth is too dry to form comprehensible words. I see the lady's name tag: "Marsha". I hope this, too, is not a bad omen. Marsha puts her hand on mine. "Oh, of course. Let me take you there. Are you feeling ok yourself, dear? You look a bit pale." I swallow hard. I am most certainly not ok. But that's not exactly what she means, and I know it. "Yes. Thank you." My voice is weak, and Marsha notices. She holds onto me as if she could help if I faint. She is frail and walks slowly, but I am sure she has more strength than I do right now.

Down one hall and then another, I look at the closed doors and wonder what is happening behind each. I try to envision babies being born. It is the only happy thing I can think might be happening right now in this place. My attempt fails though, and I know each room contains its own unique horror. Almost everyone here, except for maybe the workers, is having one of the worst days of their life.

We reach a small waiting room at the end of one of the hallways. The lights are not flickering like the one in the parking garage, but the buzzing of fluorescents is the background noise here, too. Addison sees me first and jumps up to hug me. "How bad it is?" She looks down, and I hear Marsha's slow, unsteady footsteps retreating, going to find the next lost soul to enter the building. "It isn't good, Lydia. The car hit him from behind. He flipped over his handlebars, but his shoes didn't release from the pedals right away. He rolled down an embankment." She pauses and then adds, "I'm just so glad he wasn't alone." Her voice trails, and we both know that he would not have survived even as long as he has if others were not with him.

"Can I see him?," I ask. Addison starts to answer, but a deep voice from behind responds first. "Soon. He is in surgery now, but the doctors hope he will be out in about an hour." There is a pause, and Addison grabs my hand and squeezes. My father continues, "He will be glad you came, Lydia."

30 Resistance

I'm not sure why I didn't expect him to be here. This man, our father, who has never been there for me, who has lied to me for as long as I can remember, has always been there for Alex. The emotions that rise in me are complex and numerous. They each fight to be the center of attention. Rage. Grief. Confusion. Loneliness. Relief. I am not sure which feeling to tackle first. As if it was my choice.

"Oh," is all I can say. It's a ridiculous thing to say, but it is the only thing that comes out of my mouth. "Lydia," my father pauses as if to say more, but nothing else comes forth. He is as lost as I am. I look to Addison for help, and she jumps in while maintaining her grip on my hand. "They took Alex to surgery to try to relieve some of the pressure on his brain. He has a broken hip and femur and will need many stitches." She searches for more to say. "That's all I know." Her face shows that she feels helpless. We all are helpless, all except the doctors cutting, resetting, and stitching up the only family member I have left. "We can wait together," my father says, as if to remind me that my last thought isn't quite true.

I find a seat on the opposite side of the waiting room and examine every aspect of my new surroundings to avoid seeing Gregory. It is sterile despite obvious attempts having been made to avoid this very adjective. A single muted television plays the news in one corner, closed captions scrolling along with errors in every third word or so. The hum of a vending machine pulls my attention, and I see that only two rows have offerings. Doritos, donuts, and pies chock full of preservatives weakly offer comfort for the grieving and worried patrons that fill this room on any given day. There are plastic flowers in pale blue vases, a color I know to induce calming. The chairs are padded but wipeable, and this takes away from any true sense of comfort.

I remember my phone and pull it out. There are more missed calls and texts from Zanna and Emily. *I don't remember hearing my ring tone or text alerts*, I think to myself. I open the group chat to see that Addison has thankfully let them both know that I am at the hospital, safe and sound. She fills them in with the meager details I already know, though I greedily read and reread them, hoping more understanding will come from them.

I text them myself, finally, and the responses are immediate. They share condolences and ask how I am. I do my best to put the emotion cocktail into words. My friends know me better than I know myself and respond by saying that they are on their way. I don't try to stop them. I would have felt overly dramatic asking them to join me since their presence will not heal Alex any faster or more completely, but I need them. Addison sits just a few feet away from me and responds to the group. She sends the details of where we are, and then adds, *Gregory is here, too.* There is a poignant pause that is felt even over text. I look at Addison before my phone vibrates again. *We will be right there,* Emily responds.

I go over to the doublewide seat that I know Addison chose purposefully. I lay my head on her shoulder. She doesn't say a word, but grabs my hand once more. My eyes are suddenly leaden, and I have no power left to keep them open.

I look around and see where I am. It is the same, but somehow different. The lights are the same fluorescent, and the walls the same flat white. The smell of medicine and stale coffee fills my nostrils. But then I see what is different. I am in a private room, no longer in the waiting area. Addison is gone, and the only other soul in front of me is the shell of what there once was. The steady beeping of the heart monitor and other, less steady alerts and buzzes are the only noises other than my own breathing.

My mother is so small. I move to hold her hand, but I am too afraid that the lightest of touches will break her even more than she is already broken. Her fierce hair is long gone, replaced by a scarf I found for her when I was shopping and taking a much needed break from this hospital room. It was only for an hour or so. I was too afraid to leave her for longer, scared for what I might miss.

I reach out and stroke the papery skin of her arm. Bluish green splotches cover the length of the extremity, and here too I am afraid that my touch will hurt. "Lydia." The voice is soft, barely audible, but it ignites every one of my nerve endings. "Lydia." I stand, confused. "Mom? Mommy?" She is so weak. Her eye lids are translucent, but they are still closed. "Lydia!" It is louder this time. I don't want to find it's source, now certain it is not my mother. I am pushed back into my chair. "Lydia!" I am being shaken and pulled from the last room my mother ever saw.

Emily and Zanna stare over me, gently nudging my shoulder. My eyes burn from the overhead lights, and I feel disoriented. "You got here so fast," I slur, wiping the drool that has embarrassingly run down my chin. "You've been asleep for two hours," Addison says. This knocks me out of my stupor. "Two hours!? What did I miss? Is Alex out of surgery?" I jump up and frantically try to smooth down my wrinkled clothing while heading towards the door. I don't know where I should be going, but I need to see Alex. He is probably wondering why I haven't come yet.

Emily grabs my arm to stop me. "Alex's surgery just ended. The nurse came to tell us a doctor will talk with us soon. That's why we woke you." "Oh," I say, ashamed. "I can't believe I fell asleep." I keep my eyes on the floor, too afraid to see the judgement of my friends. I should have been alert, waiting with the others, and praying. "It is normal to be overcome with exhaustion in stressful situations, Lydia. No one is upset with you." Zanna's words are kind and comforting. I think back to all of the times I slept in my mother's hospital room. It was never a sound sleep, and I was always left wanting more. After that is when my insomnia started. I thought I was finally out of that pattern, but here I am again, exhausted and finding sleep wherever I can.

A man in light blue scrubs and a scrub cap covered with an ocean scene enters the waiting room. He is shorter that I expected, though I hadn't realized I was expecting anyone in particular until right now. He has chocolate brown hair poking underneath his cap and wears a tired expression on his face that I suspect is permanent. It is then that I realize I was expecting my mother's doctor. I blink back tears and try to stay in the present.

"I'm Dr. Hendrickson. Are you all here for Alex?," the surgeon asks. "Yes," I answer first. "He's my brother." Somewhere deep inside me, I hope my attempt to publicly claim him as family will make up for how I've treated him recently. I feebly hope that this will save him. Addison's hand grips mine tighter at the sound of my words.

Dr. Hendrickson nods. "Alex made it through surgery, but he will have a long road ahead of him. I'm glad to see that he has family here." My father puts his hand on my shoulder and says, "He does. We're here for him." I instinctively shrug the hand off, and he obliges. I hope that my resistance isn't noticed by the others.

Dr. Hendrickson fills us in on the concussion, the spinal decompression that he performed, and the broken limbs that he reset. Alex hasn't woken up yet. Dr. Hendrickson is hopeful that he will, but there is no guarantee. This takes my breath away, and I am once again grateful for the group around me who would catch me should I fall at this realization. Finally, he gives the okay to see Alex, though we can only go in one at a time.

There is silence for seconds that feel like minutes. My father opens him mouth, but I talk first. "You first," I say. "He needs you more." He closes his mouth and swallows hard. I see a shine in his eyes that must mean he is holding back tears. He simply nods, puts his head down, and follows Dr. Hendrickson.

The four of us remain in the waiting room and stay quiet. Finally, I say, "He will wake up." The others look at me with tired smiles and nod, but a little too slowly. There isn't anything to say until Gregory walks back in. His eyes are red and puffy, and he is clutching a wad of tissues in his hand. "It's room 247, Lydia. It's not too far up and on your left." His eyes plead with me while mine search him. I know that he is seeing his reflection in me, and not just our similarities in this room. There is a shine in my eyes now that is most definitely tears being held back. I nod, put my head down, and search for room 247.

31 Are you ready?

Alex's body is frail. Bluish green splotches smatter every inch of exposed skin. His head has been shaved, and I can't help but picture the scarf my mother wore during her last few days on earth. The sounds and smell are unbearably familiar. *This can't be happening again.* I think of how I keep losing people. *I cannot lose him. Not when I just got him.*

I sit next to his bed and ever so carefully grab his hand. I sigh in relief when it is warm and soft, not the frigid crepe paper feeling I remember from my recent dream and not-so-distant past. Everything seems to close in, and I start to feel all of the emotions that I had been keeping at bay at once. They combine with grief for my mother, her memory so vivid within these walls. Teardrops splatter the floor, and I make no attempt to wipe them away. "Alex, please. I'm so sorry. You are my brother, and I need you. Please come back to me. We have so much to talk about. I have so much to learn from you. Please." My voice chokes on the last plea. I stay there, salt water leaving my eyes in streams, for almost an hour.

I need to share the time with Alex with Addison and Gregory. I know this, but it is hard to tear myself away. When I do, Addison takes time with her friend while I sit with Zanna and Emily. They ask how Alex looked and console me the best way they can. Gregory listens for any details that his son may be waking up, but keeps a respectful distance. Soon, he clears his throat and says, to no one in particular, that he needs to use the restroom.

When he is out of the room, Zanna and Emily exchange looks. "What?," I ask. "Lydia, you should prepare yourself for something." *There can't be more.* "What is it? Just tell me. My mother is dead, my brother may never wake up, and my estranged father is alive about 30 feet away. What else can there be?" I look back and forth between my two friends, and finally, Emily says, "Alex's mother is on her way."

I am stunned. I don't know why it did not occur to me that Alex's mother was still around. He has mentioned her, sure, but I had put her out of my mind. I hadn't processed enough to realize that I actually have a step-mother. Once again, the wind feels like it has been knocked out of me. I subtly wonder if I will suffer brain damage from so many bouts of oxygen deprivation. As soon as I think it, I feel incredibly guilty, knowing that Alex's brain function in actually in question.

"Oh," as usual for the night is all that I can think to say. I swallow hard and try to compose myself. "I forgot about her. Where was she?" It has been hours since we all arrived at the hospital, and Gregory was here before I was. "Your...um...Gregory said she was out of town visiting her sisters. She is close and will be here soon though. She called Gregory when you were in with Alex." "Oh," I reply.

Like it was timed this way, Gregory enters the waiting room at that moment. He puts his hands in his pockets and looks absolutely broken. Half of me wants him to hurt for all of the hurt I've been feeling, but the other half of me feels sympathy. His son is injured, badly, and there is nothing he can do to make it better. For the first time, I look at him fully. He stares back and waits for me to speak. Slowly, I ask, "What is your wife's name?" He seems surprised at the question. "Alma," is his one word reply. I nod and sit back in my chair.

The four of us are alone in the waiting room sitting in awkward silence. Thankfully, Addison comes back to join us, teary-eyed like Gregory and I both were not so long ago. Dr. Hendrickson is at her heels, and we all stand up, expectantly. "I haven't brought news. Alex is still the same as he was after surgery, and it is going to be a long night. Why don't you all go home and get some rest?"

"No," Gregory says adamantly. "I'd like to stay," and then less aggressively as if to save face, "if that's alright. Alex's mother will be here soon, and I'd like to be with her. We can stay through the night, just in case." Dr. Hendrickson nods. "Of course. You are welcome to visit him together when she comes. He is situated in the room now. He still shouldn't have crowds, but having family around may be helpful."

"I'll be staying, too," I offer. The others look at me, to Gregory, and back again. "I'll be fine," I tell my friends. "I need to be here. Um, as long as I can have off work tomorrow," I think to ask Addison. She lets out a small laugh and gives me a hug. "Yes, Lydia. I would never expect you to come in after this."

"I understand," says Dr. Hendrickson. *Does he?,* I wonder. I hope he doesn't. No one should have to go through this. "I will ask someone to come by with blankets and pillows for you." He turns to leave, but adds, "Alex is a lucky man to have so many people here for him."

183

A worker brings three pillows with disposable paper cases and three small throws reminiscent of airplane blankets. It will have to do, though I doubt there will be much sleeping tonight. I realize for the first time that Gregory, Alma, and I will be staying in this waiting room together, and my anxiety rises. To make matters worse, Addison, Zanna, and Emily all stand to leave together. It is late, and they are not family. Zanna whispers in my ear, "Call me if you need to get away," as she hugs me goodbye.

Gregory and I are alone in the room for less than two minutes when he abruptly stands, too quickly, and announces that he is going to the cafeteria. "Can I get you anything?," he asks. "No," I say quietly, though his offer reminds me that my stomach has been growling for some time now. "Ok. Well, I'll be right back." I just nod my head. Casual conversation was never my strong suit, but this is a whole other level. He walks out.

I turn the overhead lights out, but the room is still backlit by the television and vending machine. I hope to be asleep before Gregory returns so I can avoid him for a bit longer. I know the effort is futile, but maybe I will be able to fake sleep well enough to get the same result. I unfold the blanket and grab one of the pillows. Before I finish setting up, a woman walks in led by Marsha. Just like when she brought me, Marsha turns to go immediately.

The woman is about my height. She has dark brown, almost black hair that is a jumble of tangles. I wonder if grey is actually her natural color. She is clearly exhausted and frightened. It is how I must have looked when I walked through those doors hours before. She looks at me, and I see Alex's eyes looking back at me. "Alma," I say, without really meaning to. She looks at me, confused for only a second. "Lydia," she says, and then shares a strained, tired smile. "You know who I am?" I am surprised. *How does this whole family know about me, and I am just learning about them?* "I do know about you, but only as of recently."

Alma walks carefully over to me, as if she is approaching a wild animal. I'm sure a wild animal is exactly what I look like right now. "I'm so sorry we had to meet like this, but I am not sorry to be meeting you." She pulls me into a hug, and I find myself hugging this stranger back without hesitation. I start to cry, and she pulls me ever so slightly away so she can look into my eyes. "I'm so sorry. I can't imagine what you are feeling right now." Her kindness breaks me down even more, but I manage to choke out, "No, I'm the one who is sorry. You're here for Alex. Not me." Her face twists in pain. "I'm here for both of you." With that, we sit on the adjoined chairs where I fill Alma in on what I know about Alex. Her hand rests on mine, and I make no attempt to remove it.

Gregory returns carrying enough food to feed an army. He nearly drops it all when he sees Alma, who surprises me by not rushing into his arms. "Lydia was just filling me in," she says with her voice muted as she holds back tears. He looks at me for a moment before returning his attention to his wife. "Good. That's good. Would you like to go see him?" "Yes, please." This couple seems kind, but formal to each other, and it confuses me. Gregory starts to lead Alma to Alex's room, but stops. He lets go of her arm and picks up his cafeteria spoils that he scattered across the end table. "Here, Lydia. I know you said you didn't want anything, but," he works to find the words. "But I brought some things for you anyhow. Please, have anything you want." He returns to Alma, who looks back before leaving. "Will you be alright here? Alone?" "Yes," I lie.

When I open my eyes next, the lights are back on and there is a sideways cup of coffee in front of me. I blink several times before realizing I am the sideways one, laying down on a cramped waiting room chair. Someone had draped the thin blanket over me after I dozed off.

I sit up slowly and rub my temples. The clock on the wall reads nearly 7am. *I cannot believe I slept here.* I don't even remember laying down. I try to get my bearings and turn back to the styrofoam cup, now right side up in my vision, complete with mini creamers and sugars of all kinds. It reminds me that I'm not alone. "I didn't know how you liked your coffee, so I got one of everything they offered. But maybe you don't like coffee. I can get you tea. Do you like tea?" Gregory is talking too quickly for this hour in the morning. "The coffee is great, thanks." I add a little bit of sugar and two creamers, one vanilla and one caramel. It is hospital coffee, but it's still coffee nonetheless.

"Have there been any updates overnight?," I ask, though not hopefully. My voice is gravelly, and I work to clear it. I know that they would have woken me at night if anything changed. Both Gregory and Alma shake their heads with downcast eyes. They each share swollen, tear-stained faces, have the same exhausted look, and speak with the same tremble. But they do not share a chair. They are not holding onto each other for support. I look back and forth between them, and Alma seems to notice.

"Would you like to go see Alex together?," Alma asks me. "I would," I respond immediately, surprised by her offer as well as the bond I feel forming between us. I take a long gulp of my coffee and excuse myself to the restroom first. I try but fail to make myself look presentable. I splash water on my face and rinse my mouth with tap water. It is the best I can do for now, but I make a mental note to prioritize a trip to the gift shop for toiletries soon.

Alma and I walk to room 247 together in silence. We sit side-by-side,

Alma nearer to Alex's head. I want to respect her place as his mother, so I sit farther down by his legs. While we each sit, both in silent reflection and hope, I can't help but realize that Alma and I are in similar situations. Last night, she told me that she only recently learned about me. What must it be like to know your husband has kept this secret for all of these years?

Dr. Hendrickson interrupts my wondering. "Good morning," he says softly, trying not to startle us. "Is now a good time to talk?" Alma takes the lead. "Yes, but we should include Alex's father." I notice her choice of words, avoiding "husband". We stand slowly and head back to the waiting room where Gregory is wide-eyed and eager to hear what Dr. Hendrickson has to say. Dr. Hendrickson fills us in on the progress Alex has made over night. His cranial pressure has decreased, and his wounds are healing as well as can be expected this quickly after the injury.

"Is there a timeline we can expect?," Alma asks. Dr. Hendrickson opens his mouth to reply, but is interrupted by a nurse. "Dr. Hendrickson, can I see you please?" He excuses himself and heads to room 247. Invited or not, we all follow, Alma first, then me, and finally, Gregory.

Alma's gasp is immediate as we cross the threshold, and it doesn't take long to see why. Alex is looking over at us with his eyes opened, albeit only a slit. Dr. Hendrickson asks us to give him some space while he does a bedside neuro exam. We wait impatiently, barely daring to breathe. "Well, Alex, you gave us all quite a scare," Dr. Hendrickson says with a smile. He turns away from Alex, and we can see that he is becoming more alert by the second. "His reflexes are appropriate. This is a very good sign. I think we can safely say we are in the clear of permanent brain damage."

We all breath a collective and enormous sigh of relief. Alma grabs my hand, not Gregory's, and holds tightly. "This will still be a long road. Alex will need plenty of time to heal after his extensive injuries. He will need physical therapy as well as counseling to monitor for any PTSD from the event. We are over the first hurdle, but certainly not the last."

Dr. Hendrickson's words barely register. All I have heard is that Alex will survive this. We stay with him for as long as we are allowed, which is not nearly long enough. The doctors and nurses tell us Alex needs his rest. He isn't yet strong enough to talk, and his eyes spend more time closed than open, and we know this is true.

"Why don't you go home, Lydia?," Alma suggests. "Just for a bit. Call your friends and family, take a nap on a proper bed, and then come back." "No, thank you," I reply. I know I need this, but I'm not quite ready to leave. The medical team says Alex is stable, but I still want to be close by, at least for now. Alma smiles and says, "Let's go get breakfast then. Just the two of us, if that's alright." I shift my eyes quickly to Gregory, who looks to have aged even more over night. His eyes are still on the floor. "Alright," I accept.

Over breakfast, Alma wastes no time in addressing the elephant in the room. "How are you handling all of this, Lydia?" I assume she means the accident and the long night on the hospital couch. "I was so afraid. I feel terrible that I haven't been talking to Alex. I can't imagine losing him, especially so soon after I met him." Alma nods and shares a tired, sad smile. It is how her face has looked almost every time she has met my gaze since meeting. I can't believe that was only last night.

"I know; it's been a long several hours, but I mean with everything else. How are you handling learning about your brother and your father?"

"Oh, that." I drink my coffee to buy time and collect my thoughts. "Not well," I say, embarrassed. "It seems like you're handling it better than I did at first," Alma says as she also picks up her coffee. For the first time, I see anger in her eyes over the mug.

"I found out about a month before you did. Alex confronted Gregory and me with a picture he printed offline. He said he saw it on a posting you made. He shoved it under Gregory's nose and demanded to know if it was true. Lydia, he was so angry at both of us, but I was so confused." Alma puts down her cup and looks directly at me. "I had no idea, Lydia. None."

So Alma is struggling with her anger at Gregory. I wasn't reaching when I noticed their distance in the waiting room and again in Alex's room. "I'm so sorry. I can't imagine," I start. "You *can* imagine. And *I'm* sorry. I should have known. I should have noticed something, but I didn't....". Alma trails off, and we continue sipping our coffees in silence. Eventually, Alma asks, "Tell me about your mother. Alex said she passed but that she was a great woman."

The question surprisingly doesn't bring me pain as it usually does. Instead, I feel angry. I realize that I have given my mother a pass since she is dead, but she betrayed me too. She knew my father was alive and was content to lie to me my whole life. Alma sees the emotion behind my eyes and reaches out to me like she has done so many times since meeting me. Have we only known each other for a few hours? It feels like we came to the hospital weeks or months ago. "Don't be angry with her. Not yet. You should hear the story from Gregory first. When you're ready."

Alma is right, and I do my best to recount the best descriptions and stories about my mother. I talk about our house growing up, the smell of lilies that still brings me to her garden in my memory, reading together on the couch with our legs tangled together... Still, I can't push the anger away completely. I am exhausted with so many emotions, and Alma looks the same.

We finish breakfast and head back to the hospital. "It's time to hear the rest of the story, Lydia. Are you ready?"

32 Exhaustion, grief, and grime

I'm not ready. But as I learned from Alex's accident, tomorrows are not guaranteed. Alma and I walk into the waiting room together and see that, thankfully, the room still belongs to just the three of us. "Gregory, it's time that you tell Lydia the whole story." Gregory is surprised at this abrupt command and is visibly shaken. After a moment's hesitation, he replies, "I will, Lydia. I'll tell you anything you want. I'm so sorry. I can't forgive myself," Gregory starts, but Alma cuts him off. "We didn't ask for an apology," she snaps. "Tell her the story and then let her decide if she wants an apology." Alma pauses before turning her gaze to me. "I'm sorry, Lydia. I'm putting my own anger on you. This is your story. I'll leave so I don't talk over you."

"No!" I grab Alma's arm. "Please stay." Alma bites her lip, but agrees. "If you want me to." We both look to Gregory. He is ashen and tired. His face tells of pain. I want to feel sorry for him, but I am not ready. I need to know my story first.

"I never thought I would see you again, Lydia. I am ashamed, and I don't expect you to forgive me, but I am grateful to be able to see you. You have grown into such a beautiful young woman."

My stoic expression must tell him to get on with it.

Gregory takes a deep breath and puffs his chest out for courage. "I met your mother two years before you were born. She was waiting tables at a diner that I liked for breakfast. They had the best cinnamon French toast, and your mother would always give me extra strawberries as a topping. After coming at least once each week, your mother and I talked more and more. First, it was just about the menu, the weather...normal things like that. I would request to sit in her area, and over time, we grew to know each other as more than just a waitress and patron. Soon, I started going two or three times each week. Once I knew her schedule, I would come for dinners on her nights. I told myself it was all in good fun. We were friends. No one would get hurt if this stayed within the walls of the diner.

One night, your mother wasn't there. I was surprised to know I was hurt that she didn't tell me. I had no right to feel this way, but there it was. It was then that I knew I loved her." At this, Alma flinched. "I was engaged to Alma at the time." Gregory lowered his eyes in shame. "I told myself that I needed to choose. I wasn't the type of person to cheat, but then, I wasn't so sure it was cheating. I know now, of course, that it was, but I wasn't able to admit it to myself when I was in it.

I told myself that I wouldn't go back to the diner after that night. I stayed strong and resisted for several months. Then one morning when the sun was shining bright, I was walking past on the way...I don't remember where anymore, but I know I was walking past the window." Gregory hesitated for a beat. "I can't even say that I was going anywhere in particular if I'm being honest. I may have absentmindedly wandered to where I knew Hazel would be. I tried to look away, but your mother walked past at that exact moment. All the power in the world couldn't keep me away. I pocketed my new wedding ring and went in for just one cup of coffee. Hazel came right over to me with that toothy grin of hers and filled my cup without so much as a hello. When she turned to leave, I called out to her. After that, we talked for hours. She got in trouble with her boss, so I promised to leave her alone. She asked me to meet her after her shift. I remember fumbling with my wedding ring in my pocket, but I said yes anyhow.

I'm not proud of what I did, Lydia. I will be asking for forgiveness, even though I don't deserve it, for the rest of my life." Gregory looks towards Alma as she averts her eyes to the clock. "But I have never regretted you." I try to keep an ambivalent expression on my face, but with the exhaustion, grief, and grime that I know I wear like a blanket, I'm not sure of what this man is seeing when he looks back in my direction.

"I started living a double life. It began mostly with Alma while also dating your mother. One day not too long after, Hazel brought me back to that diner. She wasn't working there any longer, but it was still special to us. We sat together on the same side of the booth. She took my hand and put it on her stomach. That was when she told me about you. I knew then that my life would never be the same. I was so excited for you, and so was your mother. But I now had two families and knew I should come clean.

I didn't, of course. I was selfish and thought I could live two lives. I came up with a story that I told to both your mother and to Alma. I said that I got a promotion and would be traveling much more. I quietly sold every belonging that I could think of that Alma wouldn't notice. I took on extra hours at the office to do my best to keep both families afloat.
One day, when you were about five, your mother asked me to stop traveling so much. It caused arguments. She starting asking questions and began to become suspicious. Once she started looking for it, it

didn't take her long to figure me out. I came clean to her, and she broke it off. Right then and just like that. She told me that I could never come back, and that if I ever tried to contact you, she would tell Alma. I believed her, so I stayed away. I couldn't risk losing both families."

I stare at this man. This disgusting, selfish man who calls himself my father. I make no attempt to hide the hate that is filling every morsel of me.

"I came to see you when I could, when I knew that I could stay hidden. I saw your third grade play when you were a munchkin in the Wizard of Oz. I came to your middle school band recital. I was at your high school graduation, hiding in the back in the shadows." Gregory hung his head. "I don't expect you to forgive me. I was...am...a broken man with so many sins, but I never knew she told you I wasn't alive. I had no idea."

"Do not blame my mother. She did the right thing, keeping me away from you. But you could have tried harder. You should have kept trying." Even to my own ears, my words sound weak. My eyes sting with the tears I refuse to cry.

"You're right. All I can do now is say I am sorry and aim to be a better man. I will say that to you, to Alma, and to Alex, every day for the rest of my life."

I stand up and look at Alma. "I think it's time for me to go home. Will you tell Alex that I'll be back?" "Of course dear," she says, her visible grief as poignant as mine feels. I turn to leave and don't look back.

33 Angry

I stand in the parking garage and desperately search for my car. My fingers tremble as they grasp for my key fob so I can sound the alarm that will lead me to my car. I hope it will be loud and distracting, able to capture my attention for just one moment so I can find any relief from the mountain of anguish that threatens to overcome me. I find the key, and my shaky fingers press the panic button.

Nothing.

I run my fingers through my knotted hair and search for something familiar that might lead me in the right direction. Finding no beacon, I wander though the garage, slow at first and then with a quickened pace to match my frantic heartbeat. I press the panic button and hope to transfer my panic to my car. There is only silence.

A droplet hits the back of my hand. I look above, expecting to see a leak from overhead. Instead, I realize my tears could no longer be held back. The dam has broken. My panic is so extreme that I didn't even notice the streaming coming from my eyes or the sobs escaping from my throat.
BEEP BEEP BEEP

As I had hoped, this blaring sound startles me and offers a small sense of relief. I follow the alarm and flashing lights, not bothering to stop it from sounding until I am at the door. In the front seat, strapped in and ready to drive, I begin to sob once more.

Minutes or hours pass; I'm not sure which. I am all dried up. The tears from last night and today have taken every bit of moisture from me, and I am left feeling as empty as I ever have. Exhausted, I begin the drive home.

Halfway into my trek, I call my friends and relay the events of the day. The story isn't nearly as detailed as they deserve, but I tell it the best that I can. After, there is only silence. "Hello?," I ask nervously, wondering with dread if I had dropped the call and will have to retell it again once reconnected. "Wow," is Zanna's reply. "Yeah...wow," comes from Emily.

There isn't much to say, but my friends do their best to encourage me anyhow. They talk me through the rest of my drive home, more to keep me awake than anything else. When I get home, I somehow manage to get my shoes off before I collapse into bed and sleep like the dead.

I wake up angry. I am consumed. My mother. My father. My brother. My whole life. It has been a lie, and I am livid.

For the next few hours, I wrestle with my feelings. There are many, and some are conflicting. I think of Alex and feel relief in knowing he should make a full recovery. I think of Alma, and wonder how she is holding it together. I think of Gregory. Fury bubbles inside of me because of his lies, despair threatens to consume me for not being worthy of his persistent pursuit, and pity makes itself known when I think of the broken old man I saw at the hospital. And then there is my mother. I am the most angry at her, but she is the one I have the most love, respect, and grief for. These feelings are acute, and I don't know how to move forward.

Instead of wallowing, I do my best to keep moving by sheer will. I hope with all my might that it will silence the rage in my head. I shower, and it feels immeasurably good after depending on a hospital restroom for over a full day. I work to shove down the nagging feeling telling me to get back to the hospital by doing tasks that I tell myself I need to do first. I dry my hair and pull it up in a neat bun. I find comfortable capris and a soft, red baseball tee that will help me look casual but together. I brush my teeth, shape and paint my nails, and work to have the perfect combination of relaxed and sophisticated make-up. I check my phone, and a text tells me that Alex has been moved to a different room now that he is officially inpatient.

My overnight bag is repacked with all of the necessities, including ear plugs and an eye mask, though I'm hopeful that the chances of spending the night are minimal. I make myself a sandwich and fill my mug with fresh coffee. Finally, I realize that I have nothing else to do but head back to the hospital.

Instead of grabbing my keys and jetting back, I sit on my couch to collect my thoughts. In this still silence, my emotions return. Anger is the most acute, but grief continues to make itself known. Almost as soon as I allow myself to sit and feel, I find that I cannot be still. I take a deep breath and reluctantly head back to the hospital.

The car ride allows me to dwell on each emotion that I have told myself to confront one at a time. This allows me to sort and label what I am feeling, but I am no closer to resolution and I am again exhausted. This emotional roller coaster is more tiring than running a marathon. Or so I think. I have never actually done that. Feeling only slightly more clearheaded than when I last arrived, I pull in to the parking garage. I pass the same buzzing and tired light and drive past the first two or three open spots to allow myself more time walking to the hospital doors.

I flash back to the panic I felt when looking for my car. *Was that only yesterday?* I take my phone out and snap a picture of the pole near my car displaying a color-coded floor and space indicator of where I am. This time, I walk through a different, less urgent entrance. The *whoosh* of the vestibule doors sounds, and I find myself looking for Marsha. I'm surprised to realize I was hoping she would be here. She was comforting.

Instead, I follow the long beige corridor down, down, down, deep into the inpatient side of the hospital. The walls are decorated with posters of happy families meeting with models wearing scrubs. They all have white, toothy smiles and hair the picture of perfection. Each poster depicts a different hospital speciality. Pediatrics, cardiology, orthopedics, and more are displayed as if everyone within these walls will leave today whole and happy. I wonder what they would think if they heard my story.

Before I'm ready, room H8396 stands before me. I hear familiar voices inside and am relived to know Alex is awake and more alert than when I left. My body is suddenly made of ice, and I cannot move to open the door. Out here, I am still me. Inside, I am suddenly a sister, daughter, and step-daughter. I stay there for five or ten minutes, listening to the soft murmur of indistinguishable conversation. A *click* of the door startles me and suddenly, I am face to face with Addison.

"Lydia! Hi!" She folds me into a warm hug. This does the trick to thaw me and only a few seconds later, I'm able to hug her back. "I'm so glad you're back. I was just going to grab some water. Do you want me to stay and go in with you?" Her question lets me know that Gregory is inside. "Um, can I come with you to get some water? I'm thirsty." It isn't a lie. I still feel dehydrated from all of the crying.

Addison and I walk together, and I get the feeling she is taking the long way. We are mostly silent on the way other than a quick update that Alex is still weak, but that he is coherent. We fill four cups with water, one for each hand and presumably to share with Alma and Gregory, and turn to head back.

"Addison," I hesitate. She stops walking and waits. "I'm so angry." Addison nods gently and waits more. "That's it. I don't know what else to say. I'm just angry." Addison answers with a sad smile before saying, "I can't pretend to know what you're going through. But I do know that you have the chance to have a family now, if you want one. It doesn't replace your mother, but it is still a family. Maybe one day at least." I give her the same sad nod back and turn away from H8396, taking the long way back.

With Addison by my side, I have the strength to enter Alex's room. Alma and Gregory are there, one on each side of Alex's bed. Alma is holding Alex's hand and wears a relieved expression. Gregory looks like he isn't sure what to do with his hands, and his eyes dart around like he will get into trouble if he looks at one person for too long. All three look up as I enter. Alex is the first to talk. His voice sounds like his again, and his simple "Hi, Lydia" allows me to exhale the breath I didn't know I was holding.

"You're awake." It's a silly thing to say. Alex is clearly awake, and I knew that since yesterday. Somehow though, this feels more real. He feels more solid. Alma and Gregory seem to take that as a cue to go for a walk, and Addison steps out with them.

"You scared me," I say. Alex gives a weak chuckle. "I scared myself." I squeeze his hand as we sit quietly for a minute or two. The silence is comfortable. It allows a tiny bit of my anger to dissipate. The room is chilly, and I'm grateful that I didn't choose to wear a short sleeved shirt. The TV on the wall plays Seinfeld without sound. The blinds are drawn so that all of the light in the room is unnatural. A movable table has leftover lunch that has barely been touched; only a few bites of tomato soup are gone, and a packet of crackers is empty.

"You didn't eat much," I try to say as Alex simultaneously blurts out, "I'm so sorry." "We don't have to talk about that now." I'm afraid to get him worked up, and I know this could be an upsetting conversation. "We do, Lydia. What if I fall out of my bed and go into a coma tonight?" I gasp, but Alex is smirking. "Don't even joke!" He laughs at me, and I feel the need to swat him with a pillow. The moment feels like it should with a big brother, and the thought sobers me.

"I was so mad at you, Alex. And then you go and get hit by a car."

"Yeah, well, I couldn't get you to answer me any other way." Again I gasp, and Alex smirks. He backpedals when I don't soften my expression. "That was another joke, but I guess it was a bad one." "No kidding!," I snap. "Ok, joking aside," he continues, "I'm really sorry. I should have told you when I found out. I should have dealt with it with you rather than try to sort it out alone first. I guess," he pauses and looks away. "I guess I felt protective of you. I knew how hurt I was. I knew you would be hurt even more. I wanted to hold off on the pain I knew would come."

My throat tightens and my vision blurs. I work to push the lump in my throat down, then take several deep breaths to stop the tears.

"Thank you," I mumble, almost inaudibly. "Thank you?," he gawks. "Yes, thank you." I collect my thoughts. "I was so mad at you. But I think it was just easier to feel mad at you than to deal with it. Thank you for trying to protect me. This isn't your fault."

Alex squeezes the hand I forgot he was holding. We both turn to the television and watch Kramer silently slide into the apartment and pretend like we haven't seen the episode ten times before. It breaks for commercial, and Alex starts again. "You don't have to forgive him, you know. I would understand. And so would my mother." He says the last part more harshly. "It's a lot to have sprung on her, too." "I know," he says. "It doesn't make the fighting any easier. I know I'm not an eight year old child whose parents might split, but I still hate it. She has been staying at my aunt's for a while. I wonder what this accident will do. I hope it doesn't make things worse." I'm not sure what to say. Sometimes stress like this accident brings people together, and sometimes, when you're already fragile, it tears them apart.

Instead of trying to tackle any more life changing drama, we catch up on the parts of our lives we have missed over the past few weeks. He tells me about the accident and the rides and hikes I missed. I tell him about working with Addison. As if she heard her name, and I suspect she did, a light rap on the door tells us she is going to join us. The three of us laugh and chat like old friends, and I finally feel like I can breathe again.

34 Shake your pompoms

Summer turns to fall, and I spend my time split between *Wasatch Wonder*, my apartment, and visiting Alex during his intensive physical therapy. He is healing slowly, a reminder that we are no longer 18 years old. As his breaks and fractures mend, Alex progresses from sitting up, to using light hand weights, and finally, to pushing himself in a wheelchair.

On this particular Thursday, I show up to Alex's PT with childlike pompoms that you can buy at the dollar store or are given for free at most sporting events. I found the green and white novelties while shopping the other day and knew I had to have them. I arrive just a few minutes past the start of therapy so I know that Gregory will not be there any longer.

On Thursdays, we have the unspoken rule that Gregory brings Alex and then leaves so I can come to support Alex without the added anxiety. Sure, Alex and I have discussed the situation in depth, starting with his sympathetic disdain for the man he calls Dad. We progressed to agreeing to disagree, as he assured me it's ok to be angry while also filling me in on all of the times Gregory *was* there. For Alex. Not for me. Last week, he shared how his father was so proud to see him toss his mortar board when he graduated college and then of the worn-down grey Buick he bought him to celebrate. I know what he is doing. Alex is working to paint the picture of a man who *was* there. One who wiped his tears after he fell and cheered loudly when he scored the winning run. All I am hearing is of what this man was doing when I was alone with a single parent.

Alex laughs when he sees my cheerleader paraphernalia. I wave from across the room as I pull a chair nearer to where Alex is getting his legs stretched by his therapist. His grimaces from working his legs in a way he so desperately misses. I feel a tap on my shoulder and look up to see Addison. "I hope it's ok that I came today," she says in a whisper. Alex hears despite her quiet voice and looks over with a big grin. He changes his demeanor from unabashed discomfort to dedicated determination.

Addison and I catch up on our day at the store experienced from two different vantage points. I describe the young couple excited to bring home Addison's portrait of Powder Mountain at dusk, complete with miniature skiers calling last run. She tells me of the vase she is forming to look like a waterspout she saw last weekend.

Addison goes suddenly quiet, and I follow her gaze to the parallel bars where Alex is pensively looking forward. The air seems to go out of the room as Alex reaches for the arm of his chair, shaking. I silently hand Addison a pompom in preparation to celebrate what is unfolding before us. Alex plants one food clad in hipster-style white Keds on the floor. The other follows and both hands move to take his weight on the bars.
Alex takes a step.

Addison and I reach out for each other but stay completely quiet. Two steps are complete. Alex pants and yells, "You guys are too quiet!". His icebreaker causes us to laugh, and that seems to propel him two more steps forward quickly. The tiny burst of speed causes him to stumble, but instead of silently gasping as he obviously does not appreciate, Addison and I shake our pompoms aggressively and shout encouragements. A flicker of a smile adds to the strain painted on Alex's face, and it seems to carry him along. Four more slow steps, and he is at the end of the pathway, collapsing into a waiting chair.

That is the cue we need to rush over and shower Alex in hugs and plastic threads of green and white. He pants and laughs while Addison and I sigh a breath of relief. Alex has walked again.

His therapist gives him a short break, but soon, he is back to strength work. Alex is not a quitter, and this taste of self ambulation has clearly inspired him to work even harder. Forty minutes later, Alex is drenched in sweat, and Addison and I congratulation him on such a huge accomplishment. I say my goodbyes just a few minutes earlier than Addison and Alex do.

In the comfort of my car, I watch as Gregory walks inside while Alma waits by the car door. He looks less broken than he did when I saw him at the hospital, and he is certainly stronger than when I said goodbye only to Alex and Alma when Alex was discharged. Only a minute or two later, he walks next to Alex as Alex pushes himself down the ramp and to their car. Alma is standing and waiting to help Gregory get Alex into the car. Each weak, the two team-lift Alex while he uses his own growing upper body strength to get him in this car.

Tonight is different. Gregory opens the door to the backseat, and Alma reaches to help lift him. Alex puts his hand up and must say something, because his parents take a very small step back. He slowly and shakily pushes up, puts one foot down, then an arm on the car door, and then the other foot down. I see Alma's arms fighting against her mind as they continue to jut out to help her son, and then just as quickly pull back to let him do it himself. Gregory is better at standing back, I notice with annoyance that is probably unwarranted. Alex gets himself into the car.

Alex has taken this one giant step back towards independence, and I smile big for him. I watch the family, which I remember is also my family, pull away. In the habit I have followed every week so far, I turn my lights on only after they are out of the parking lot. Only then do I start the drive home.

I am happy to know that I now seem to have a better balance in my life. I sit on my couch, curled up in the same plush blanket that has comforted me so many evenings before, and read about Mr. Darcy and Elizabeth for the third time. I am able to focus more on reading, but I am able to live outside of the pages as well. I send Zanna and Emily a text update of the day's progress, and they are overjoyed that Alex is continuing to heal.

Just as I sit back to sigh with relief and satisfaction, my phone *pings*. Expecting another comment from Zanna, I'm momentarily surprised to see Alex's name on my screen. Having him in my life is so much better than being angry with him. We are planting the seeds of being siblings. The process is simultaneously easy, since we are friends again, as well as challenging, while we try to fill these roles that we each have gone decades not considering.

Tonight was a big night!

It was! I'm so happy for you. How do you feel now?

Exhausted, like I hiked 14 miles and then biked 20 up the steepest

Wasatch peak.
I bet. You did so good! You'll be running again in no time.

Ha...we'll see.   *So....*

So?

So, my parents want to throw a small party to celebrate on Saturday. I would love it if you could come.

That's great they're throwing you a party!

Don't deflect, Lydia. Addison will be there and you can bring Zanna and Emily. Will you be there? It would mean a lot.

I don't know. Can I think about it?

Come on! Don't make me grovel. I'll pull the "I almost died" card!

How annoying of him. I know this is a big deal, and he's right, I can't say no to this. I will bite the bullet to make up for being a bad sister and friend before the accident.

I'll be there.

35 Catching my breath

My blankets are cocooned around me as I lay in my comfort spot, my couch, and wonder how I will get through the day. My eyes search the photograph showing the young Gregory's sandy blonde hair and emerald eyes that are the precise shade of mine. My focus shifts to Alex's blue eyes and slender nose that are now obviously from Alma. My imagination adds to the scene, complete with the moving truck, bright blue mailbox, and charming cottage-style house with white shutters and a door painted the same shade of blue to match the mailbox. I close my eyes to feel the early spring air and smell the blossoms on the trees in the yard.

I now believe this scene to be the last straw for my mother. I imagine her finding this picture that proved my father's double life. I replay the scenes of my mother crying in my mind, the recent dreams that were born from buried memories, and know that it is all true. My mother lied to me for my whole life. My father left and barely tried to find me. I pull the covers over my head and squeeze my eyes shut, trying to turn off my mind.

It doesn't work. Instead, I see the way my life would have been with a father. But I also see how it would have been for Alma and Alex. My mind drifts to the days of laying in the grass, watching the clouds with my mother. We were happy and at peace. A thought strikes me that the decisions that both of my parents made caused the rest of my life to happen as it did. I would have changed my marriage, and I certainly would have changed my mother's cancer, but I can honestly say that I wouldn't change anything else. These decisions, as horrible as they were, brought me to where I am today. They helped shape me into who I am today. I am Lydia Alecia, and I am strong.

I peel back my covers and blink back the sunlight. In slow motion, I unfold myself from the couch nest that I have made and stand to stretch. I lay the picture down on my table and start some coffee. While it brews and the rich aroma fills the air, I change into shorts and a tank top so I can head to the gym.

I have been trying to keep some of the fitness I gained with Alex and Addison, and I want to be ready to join them again at the next opportunity. I know Alex will be a bit behind me, but we can motivate each other. The rhythmic movement and music in my ears will help to prepare me for the strain of the afternoon to come.

I need to let go of the anger that is only holding me back. I have so many questions that I wish I could ask my mother, but that will never happen. The truth is, I now have three new family members who I can talk with. I know it will be a process, but having so much anger has only stunted me. I need to move forward.

At precisely 2:30pm, there is a knock at my door. I let out a huge sigh of relief to know that I am not alone. The door opens to Zanna and Emily greeting me with hugs and a handful of lilies. *I have never been alone*, I think gratefully. The lilies are a beautiful creamy white and have a scent that is the closest thing to a hug from my mother that I can get.

"I am so happy you're coming to Alex's party with me." "We wouldn't have it any other way," Emily says with a touch at my arm. I can tell by this motion and the look in her eyes that she is concerned for me. There has been so much constant change for so long now. She knows that I have been fragile.

"I had some clarity today," I tell my friends. I share my realization that while the lies and poor choices were not what I would have hoped for, they did give me the life that I had. Despite so many struggles for more than a year, I really have a great life. This life includes the two strong and selfless ladies standing before me. I tell them that I am ready to *try* to move on, and that starts with letting go of the anger. "It doesn't help. It just hurts me more."

Our trio pulls up to a suburban two-story home with a wrap-around porch. It is charming and not overly large. The home is well kept with perfectly trimmed shrubs lining the porch and side-by-side pristine white rocking chairs displaying matching pillows that say "home" and "love". Zanna comments, "It's a little much, don't you think? The pillows?" "Thank goodness you said it," I sigh in relief. "I wasn't sure if I was being too harsh or not." Emily just laughs in agreement while she does her best not to insult anyone.

Addison greats us as the door, carrying an oversized bottle of champagne and five red Solo cups. "Thank goodness!," Zanna says emphatically. She wastes no time in handing out the cups but pauses at the fifth cup. "Over here," comes a voice that is stronger than I expected. We round the corner to the other side of the porch where hanging flowers and more wooden rocking chairs greet us. Alex is smiling while holding his hand out for a cup. "Ah, the man of the hour," I say and lean down for a hug.

Addison pops the cork, and our new group made up of family and friends cheers while the bubbly pours over. Zanna darts her hand out to catch the overflowing liquid. "Relax!," Addison laughs. "There is plenty more inside." She pours our favorite drink for each of us, and we clink our plastic cups together. "To new beginnings," says Addison as she holds her plasticware to the middle of our circle. "To new beginnings," the rest of us agree. I catch the look between Addison and Alex lasting longer than I expect. Zanna and Emily must too, because they both look over at me with barely veiled surprise. We shrug and enjoy a sip that feels long overdue.

The celebration between the five of us lasts only a few minutes. The creek of an opening door causes us all to turn expectantly towards the house. The sunset from behind adds an element of beauty and calm to the scene while we wait to see who is joining us.

Gregory turns the corner, a look of hope mixed with fear in his eyes. He has his own cup in one hand and another opened bottle of champagne in the other. "I thought one bottle wouldn't be enough for all of you, especially if you were interested in allowing one more to join you." He looks cautiously to me, waiting for his invitation in such a nervous way that he doesn't seem presumptuous. The others wait for my response in silence, knowing it is my call.

I grab the nearly empty first bottle and pour the remaining contents into Gregory's cup. "It's nice to see you, Gregory." He takes a sharp breath in while a tear enters his eye. He nods ever so slightly, and I clink my cup to his. The rest join in. I look around and smile at my friends and my family. I can finally catch my breath.

Epilogue

I'm not one to believe in happy endings. They seem unrealistic and hokey. But here we are. The sun is warm on my bare shoulders, and my dress billows around my legs. Green is a good color for me. It complements my hair, which has had its ringlets tamed and is now perfectly positioned with floral clips. The wrap-around porch is decorated with lilies, and the same flowers make up my petite bouquet. I breathe in easily and embrace the scent surrounding me. The clouds overhead are picturesque, and I can almost see my mother smiling through them at me. I smile back and give her a silent "thank you" for the life she allowed me to build.

The music cues my steps, and a handsome man sporting aviators holds out his arm for mine. We walk slowly down the aisle, smiling at the gathering of happy faces whom I have grown to know and love over these past two years or so. Emily and Zanna smile at me from their seats, families in tow.

I turn my gaze forward and see my brother's anxious and eager smile looking back at me. I take my place up front, next to but not too close to Alex, and smile warmly back at him. Cannon in D begins to play, softly at first, and then with a crescendo that cues us all to stand. Before looking back down the aisle like everyone else, I look first at

211

Alex. His anxiousness has disappeared, replaced by love in every definition of the word. I find Alma and Gregory, hand in hand in the front row. They have been through so much these past few years, and I am relieved to see them together and stronger than ever. Their eyes are proud as they, too, look at Alex first.

I then join the congregation to watch the beautiful bride walk the aisle, radiant under her glistening veil. At the front, her father raises the veil, kisses her cheek, and hands her off to Alex. Addison offers me her bouquet that is an eloquent display of color and white. Knowing that Addison created this herself makes it even more special. I smile at my friend, my soon to be sister-in-law, and I am filled with such happiness, love, and togetherness that I had not known existed until only recently. I breathe easily and watch as yet another new beginning unfolds before me.

Acknowledgements

Thank you so much for reading *Four Hundred Sycamore*! I had such a great time writing it, and I wouldn't have been able to do it without my editor, cheerleader, and fiancé, Jeff O'Donnell. I am so grateful for you!

A HUGE thank you to my readers! I hope you enjoyed Lydia's trials and growth and were able to draw strength from her.

Please check out my children's book titled *A Little Birdie Told Me*: In *A Little Birdie Told Me*, we follow a young bear who is struggling to hear his family, friends, and teachers. Throughout the story, our bear friend finds out about his hearing loss from an audiologist and learns of the exciting world of sound through his new, colorful hearing aids. The bear's friend, "a little birdie," joins him throughout his journey. *A Little Birdie Told Me* is available through Amazon.

Made in the USA
Middletown, DE
23 December 2021

56627984R00128